I heard a sound behind me. And then there were strong hands against the small of my back, shoving me forward with brutal force, propelling my body straight into the wall of the closest building. Fingers wrapped themselves around my wrist—the hand that still held the silver weapon—slamming it up against the building once, twice, three times. I heard a sharp *crack,* felt a searing pain, even as I heard the silver clatter to the sidewalk.

"Look at me. Look at me, you stupid little bitch," a voice rapped out.

I looked. And found myself staring straight into the second vampire's eyes. Dark as midnight, as the lowest level of Hell. In them, I saw precisely what he wanted me to see: my own death.

Also by Cameron Dean

PASSIONATE THIRST
LUSCIOUS CRAVING

Eternal Hunger

A CANDACE STEELE
VAMPIRE KILLER NOVEL

CAMERON DEAN

BALLANTINE BOOKS · NEW YORK

A Ballantine Books Mass Market Original

Copyright © 2006 by Parachute Publishing, LLC
Excerpt from *Passionate Thirst* by Cameron Dean copyright © 2006 by Parachute Publishing, LLC

Published in the United States by Ballantine Books, an imprint of The Random House Publishing Group, a division of Random House, Inc., New York.

BALLANTINE and colophon are registered trademarks of Random House, Inc.

ISBN 978-0-345-49255-5

Cover illustration and design by Tony Greco

Printed in the United States of America

www.ballantinebooks.com

OPM   9 8 7 6 5 4 3 2 1

For Sharon and Dana. Eternal love.

Eternal Hunger

One

It was a stormy night.

I live in Vegas, so I can't exactly claim that it was dark, too. I can, however, say this much.

There's better weather in Hell.

The rain came down in solid sheets, the drops just short of hail but still hard enough to sting with cold. The wind was straight out of a late-night horror film, an unseen force that should not be sentient but still manages to have a mind of its own; pushing against me with invisible hands, tearing at my clothing, howling through the city like a long-lost soul. It was the sort of night when anyone with half a brain cranks up the knob on the gas fireplace, slips their favorite DVD into the machine, and curls up on the couch.

So what was I doing? I was pounding the streets of Vegas, soaked to the skin, tracking someone who probably thought the weather was nice.

My name is Candace Steele and I hunt vampires.

Usually I do this indoors. I work undercover security at one of the newest casinos in town, the Scheherazade. I look like a thousand other females in Vegas, serving drinks and flashing some skin. But in fact I'm one of a kind. Because while I'm making my rounds, I'm also doing something else: spotting vampires. Getting them tossed out on their undead asses if they try to cheat the casino by manipulating the minds of the humans around them, a technique vampires call "establishing rapport." This happens to be something they enjoy. A lot. Trying to get the better of humans, I mean. Which pretty much means my job is never dull.

It doesn't make my days off uninteresting, either. And it definitely explains what I was doing out in the weather on this awful night.

The original plan was to go to a movie. I almost got there, too, actually ducking under the cover of the theater awning. Then I felt it: a surge of cold straight down my back—one I knew damn well had nothing to do with the storm.

There was a vampire nearby.

I concentrated, trying to zero in on my own sensations. The cold felt odd, somehow. Usually when I sense a vampire is near, once the cold kicks in, it's a constant presence. The intensity of the cold tells me the strength of the vampire. But this time the cold faded in and out in a strange sort of ebb and flow. Each time it returned, it got a little stronger, almost as if it were being reinforced.

Oh, God, I thought. *Oh, no.* There is just one way for a vampire to reinforce its power: by consuming the blood of something alive. Unless I very much missed my guess, the something alive in this case was a human being. And it wouldn't be alive for very much longer.

In spite of human fears and assumptions to the contrary, not all vampires feed on human beings. Only those in the upper echelons, the big guns. Or, on occasion, lower-level vampires with special permission from the higher-ups. I didn't think the vampire whose trail I was attempting to pick up at the moment was one of those. The cold was too intense, too strong. I left the movie theater, following the cold beyond it to the corner, then took an involuntary step back as the wind shoved me. A sudden splatter of raindrops pelted across my face like a handful of thrown pebbles. They stung.

By now my adrenaline was starting to kick in as my vampire-hunting instincts took over. I didn't know yet whether I'd be in time to save tonight's human victim, but I could at least promise one thing by way of consolation: I'd make sure the vampire didn't make it, either. There would be one less bloodsucker before the night was done.

As if on cue, there was a flash of lightning, a clap of thunder almost directly overhead, and then the rain came down even harder. I flipped up the collar on my jacket in a feeble attempt to keep the rain from streaming down the back of my neck, slid one of the silver wands I always use to help control my wayward hair into my jacket pocket, and kept on going, hot on the trail of the cold.

Vampire Hunter Rule #1: Never, under any circumstances, go out into the world unarmed. Rule #2: When in doubt, make silver your weapon of choice. Silver is a purifier. A little goes a long way when it comes to vampires.

By the time I reached the far end of the block, I was completely soaked. The wind was so strong I had to lean into it, as if walking up an incline. But the internal cold I felt still pulled me forward, steady as a lodestone. I crossed the street, stepped up onto the curb, and saw the vampire.

He was young—not more than early twenties—and wearing a muscle T-shirt and skintight jeans that had probably been plastered to his body even before the rain got to them and finished the job. As he stepped out from under the cover of a parking garage not twenty paces away, oblivious to the weather, he looked entirely too pleased with himself, with his own power. *New kid on the block,*

I thought. *On a feeding high.* His eyes slid over me, barely registering my presence. I felt my adrenaline kick up a notch. My biggest weapon in my fight against vampires isn't anything I carry with me, anything external. It's me. The fact that, unaccustomed to humans being able to detect what they are, most vampires literally never see me coming.

As if to prove he was no different from the rest, the vampire in question pivoted on one black-booted heel and began to walk away; his arrogance and enjoyment of his own power showing in every step. It might have been a balmy summer night for all the notice he took of the weather. I waited until he was half a block away, then sprinted for the entrance to the parking garage.

The interior was dark as a tomb, appropriate considering the fact that it was now the temporary resting place of something no longer alive. I moved past the entrance, stopped, turned back, swore viciously as the wind blew against me and the rain came down. Every instinct I had was screaming at me to follow the vampire. Don't lose sight of the quarry. Don't let the enemy get away. But if I did that, I would do precisely the same thing the vampire had: I'd put him first, and the human being second. That was a choice I simply could not make and still face myself in the morning. Before I could run the vampire to ground, I had to make absolutely certain I knew the fate of the human being he had left behind.

Well, shit, I thought. "Shit, shit, shit," I muttered under my breath as I ducked into the parking garage. At least I was out of the rain. I gave the lapels of my jacket a quick shake to lose as much water as I could, then fished my keys out of my pocket, activating the mini-flashlight that hangs on the end of the chain. It didn't exactly illuminate a lot of area, but even a little was better than nothing.

It was the cards that helped me find her. You see them all over Vegas, littering the sidewalks like X-rated confetti. *Experience the Best of Vegas. Full service 24/7.* I found a whole pile of them at the end of the first row of cars, all with the same picture on them. A slim, young blonde with a phone number covering her naked, upthrust breasts. Her eyes were on the camera, but her head was thrown back, exposing a long, white neck. A choice that had probably seemed sexy at the time. *Nichole,* the card read. *Blond. Sweet. Very Petite.*

Also, very, very dead.

She was sprawled across the hood of the last car in the row, spread-eagled on her back, skirt hiked up to expose her thighs. A position that left little doubt as to how vampire guy had talked her into ducking in here in the first place. Her big blue eyes were wide open and sightless. Her face was still beautiful, but her long white neck was a mess. I could say it was a bloody mess, but that would be a lie. There wasn't a drop of blood, not anywhere. A circumstance that would no doubt convince the cops, when they finally arrived, that sweet, petite Nichole had been killed somewhere else, then dumped in the parking garage. But I knew better. I knew the truth. She had been killed precisely where she lay, by a killer who had taken every single drop of blood he could get his fangs on.

It wasn't until I saw the beam of the flashlight waver that I realized I was crying and shaking with pain and outrage. I guessed Nichole was no older than eighteen. That undead SOB had treated this girl like a fast-food meal and then threw away the wrapper that was her body. I couldn't save her. I was way too late for that. But I could get even—for her, for all of us who live and breathe. I could still make him pay.

I took another thirty seconds to place an anonymous call to 911. I resisted the impulse to lean over and ease her eyelids closed. Then I went back out into the storm.

* * *

I picked up the vampire's trail about three blocks away. Either I'd taken less time in the parking garage than I'd feared, or this vampire wasn't in much of a hurry. By the time I made it back outside, the rain had slacked off a little, as if the cloud carrying the initial burst had moved on. Thank God for small favors. But the wind was still bitterly cold. The vampire kept to the secondary streets, off the Strip, strutting like John Travolta in *Saturday Night Fever*, really reveling in his power, feeling his oats. It would have been laughable if the reason for his behavior hadn't made me so angry. And if I wasn't so damned wet and cold. My jeans clung to my legs like leeches. The inside of my thighs felt raw where the thick fabric rubbed them. My socks sloshed inside my boots with every step I took.

For ten endless blocks, I trailed the vampire until I wanted to take him out for no other reason than to take myself out of the wet and the cold. *Come on*, I urged him silently. *Make your move, you undead creep. Turn off. Show me where you're going.* The street we were on was still way too public to risk a confrontation, even given the storm.

Do something, Candace, I thought. *Stop following him like some lovesick schoolgirl and make something happen.* If the vampire wasn't going to give me the opportunity I wanted, I was just going to have to make one of my own.

I quickened my pace, sliding a second wand of silver from my hair, tucking it into my left-hand jacket pocket. I had a silver spike ready and waiting for either hand now. At once, soggy curls flopped down into my eyes. Through them, I could see the vampire pausing on the corner beneath a streetlight, waiting for the signal to change. I felt a bubble of laughter rise inside my chest; I fought it down. He had no trouble ripping some girl's throat out, but he obeyed the traffic laws. I picked up my pace again. I was running now, my feet heavy against the rain-slicked sidewalk.

Come on, I urged him. *Hear me coming.*

Precisely as if obeying my command, he turned around. I let my momentum carry me forward, crashing into him, clutching at him as if he were a lifeline. I pulled him around the corner, onto the side street.

"Oh, thank goodness," I sobbed out. "I'm so glad I found someone."

"Whoa," the vampire said, and then smiled. In the time it had taken our bodies to connect, he had come to the conclusion I posed no threat. How could I? I was only human, after all. Sure, I could have just nailed him right away and been done with it, but that wasn't what I wanted. I wanted to toy with him a little, work him around to just one moment when he could see the end of his existence coming. See it and be powerless to stop it. It wasn't much to offer sweet, petite Nichole, but I had to figure it was better than nothing.

"I'm being followed. I think I'm being followed," I gasped out, letting my words tumble over one another even as I leaned into him. I felt his arm snake around my waist to hold me close. If anyone saw us, we'd look like two sweethearts hurrying to get out of the rain.

"Please, you've got to help me," I pleaded. "I'm new to Vegas. I'm just a tourist. I got lost—in the storm—I lost my way." I began to pull at him, urging him away from the street corner as if expecting my pursuer to burst into view at any minute. My goal was the center of the block, where the spill from the streetlights left a dark band of shadow.

"Of course I'll help you," the vampire said. "Woman like you shouldn't be on her own. Vegas can be a dangerous town. But you don't have to worry. You can trust me."

In a pig's eye, I thought.

"Oh, thank you," I sobbed out. I stopped moving, dropped my head against his chest as if overwhelmed with relief. "You can't imagine what it feels like to find somebody kind. I've been so frightened. You have no idea."

"First thing we do is get you out of the rain," he said. "And out of those wet clothes."

You are such an asshole, I thought. *Pouring down rain, damsel in distress, and what do you do? You hit on her.*

I giggled then, as if he had actually said something original, and gave a shiver that insinuated me a little closer to his body. I couldn't exactly claim I pressed my breasts against his chest, considering they were covered by my jacket, but it wasn't for lack of trying.

"I just feel so confused," I confessed. "Like I'm having a panic attack or something. I can't even remember which is the way to my hotel. If I could just be somewhere safe, I'm sure I'd get my bearings back. I'm just so scared, so cold."

"Not to worry," the vampire said easily. "My place isn't far."

It never is, I thought.

"What if he's seen us?" I exclaimed suddenly. I jerked backward, out of the vampire's arms. Instantly, he reached for me, but I scooted out of range. I was in the darkest part of the block now. I wrapped my arms around myself, hugging my elbows, then slid my right hand down and into my jacket pocket. "I could get you in trouble. You might even get hurt. I couldn't bear it if that happened. I would never forgive myself."

"You don't have to worry about that," the vampire said, his voice soothing. He followed me into the shadowy center of the block. He reached for me again, and this time I let him bring me close. Palming the silver, I wrapped my arms around his back. He tilted my face up, brushed the water from my cheeks. "Trust me. I can handle anything that comes along."

"Can you really?" I asked, my voice breathless, as if we were standing together on a night drenched with moonlight instead of wind and rain. I watched the cockiness come into his face.

"You don't have to worry about a thing," he said.

I slid my hand up his back, and jammed the silver straight into the side of his neck.

"You know what?" I said. "You're absolutely right."

I had it then—the moment I'd been waiting for. His eyes went wide with horrified comprehension, his mouth made a round O of astonishment and pain. And then he crumbled into dust.

As I watched him disintegrate, I heard a sound. Behind me. Sibilant, leathery, vaguely familiar, but not readily identifiable. And then there were strong hands against the small of my back, shoving me forward with brutal force, propelling my body straight into the wall of the closest building. Fingers wrapped themselves around my wrist—the hand that still held the silver—slamming it up against the building once, twice, three times. I heard a sharp *crack*, felt a searing pain, cried out even as I heard the silver clatter to the sidewalk. In the next instant, the hands released my wrist to tangle in my sodden hair, propelling my head forward against the building so hard that I saw stars. Blood erupted from my nose.

Cold, I thought. *I'm so very, very cold.*

I knew then what I would see as my attacker spun me back around. He shook me, my head flopping, my neck as limp as a rag doll's.

"Look at me. Look at me, you stupid little bitch," a voice rapped out.

I looked. And found myself staring straight into a second vampire's eyes. Dark as midnight, as the lowest level of Hell. In them, I saw precisely what he wanted me to see: my own death.

Sheer instinct took over then as adrenaline flooded through me, pushing back even the bone-chilling cold. I was Candace Steele. I'd faced strong vampires before. I was not going down without a fight. I slapped at him, desperately trying to gain even a little room to maneuver, then screamed as pain from my broken wrist sang up my arm. He laughed, backhanded me viciously, releasing his hold on me at the same time. My head snapped sideways and back, connecting with the wall once more. My vision went stark white, then gray around the edges. My ears roared with sudden sound. Slowly, I began to sink down against the wall, my only support. Before I hit the sidewalk, the vampire reached down, seized the lapels of my jacket, and hauled me upright. He yanked the jacket open as if the leather were a dry corn husk, grabbed my hair, pulled my head to one side.

And then his teeth were in my throat.

My whole body spasmed, arching up on a great wave of pain. My lips opened in a silent cry. My hands scrabbled against his back, trying to gain some sort of hold to pull him away from me. He made a sound like an animal and I swear I felt the grip of his teeth tighten, gnawing at my neck like some feral dog. My knees buckled and my legs gave way. Slowly, locked together in our terrible embrace, we sank to the wet sidewalk.

His teeth never relinquished their hold on my neck as he shifted position, turning so that his back was against the wall now. Supporting me as I slid to the ground, cradling me in his lap as a loving parent might a child. Sounds seemed to magnify inside my head. The sound the rain made against the leather of my jacket, different from where it hit the sidewalk. The even, steady rhythm of the vampire's swallows as he drank my blood. My ears rang, then began to pound. Thum *thump*. Thum *thump*. Thum *thump*. *My heart. That is my heart,* I thought. Desperately beating, trying to keep me alive. It wasn't going to work. Nothing was going to work.

I was going to die.

I had a strange, crystalline moment then, a moment out of time. Even as sensation began to leave it for good, I felt my whole body, every single part of it, for the very last time. My butt against the vampire's lap, my shoulders and head where they rested against his supporting shoulder and arm. My legs, stretched straight out in front of me, extending past him to rest on the wet sidewalk. The throb of my broken wrist, trapped between us. My head, turned away, facing out toward the street. My left arm extending into space, the hand, palm up. As if they belonged to a stranger, I watched the fingers move, and it seemed to me that they were trying to tell me something. My body was getting it backward, and my hand was trying to give my brain a command. There was something the hand should do. Something important.

Just go for it, I thought. The world was a sea of shades of gray, like an old black-and-white television show. I watched as my pale gray fingers trembled, then jerked toward the darker gray that was the closest jacket pocket. My hand fumbled there for precious, endless seconds, then found its way inside. And, at that moment, my brain caught up. It knew what it was supposed to do now. It was supposed to save me.

In that pocket was my other silver wand.

I felt my fingers close around it and, for one blinding second, there was color in the world once more. A haze of red pain so bright and vicious it made me scream even with the vampire's teeth embedded in my throat. My hand jerked, straight out, the silver wand clutched in my fist. My arm shot straight up. Then, as if those two motions had exhausted my last strength, my arm began to fall back down. Against all odds, I felt the tip of the silver wand catch, then drag as my arm descended.

The teeth in my throat let go as the vampire opened his mouth to howl, a furious, inhuman sound. He released me, shoving me from him with a violence so sudden I tumbled over backward, the back of my head bouncing against the sidewalk like a rubber ball. Stars wheeled before my eyes. Gorgeous, silver, sparkling. They reminded me of something. A thing that made me want to weep and sing, all at the same time.

And then even they disappeared and the only thing that existed in the world was the rain, falling down into my open, sightless eyes.

Two

When I knew myself once more, I was in the dark, but a kind of dark I almost didn't recognize. Backward, just like my hand and brain had been. Not external, but coming from somewhere deep inside my own form. The outlines of my surroundings loomed around me, but they were shapes only, impressions in a fog. I could no longer feel the wind or rain. *Inside,* I thought. *Out of the storm.* A living room, perhaps. I was lying on my side on what I thought must be a couch. A low table sat alongside. I tried to reach for it, but found I couldn't move. I had the desire, but not the strength, to make my body function.

"Candace," I heard a voice say. "*Candace.*" And it seemed to me suddenly that I'd been hearing it all along. This was what had called me back to even this shadowy world. This voice, saying my name over and over. Begging, swearing, pleading. This set of arms, holding me as if they'd never let go. I felt them lift me, shake me, and in that moment the pain roared through me, hot enough to scald. I wasn't dead then. Not yet. Agony belongs to living beings. Against all odds, I was still alive.

"Candace," the voice said, once more. "You've got to look at me. You've got to focus. We haven't much time."

I blinked rapidly, desperately trying to clear my vision, and suddenly the dark was full of stars. They danced and wavered, then narrowed down to two. Two. His eyes.

"Ash," I said. Forcing the single syllable through my throat was like swallowing ground glass. Ash, the vampire I hated. Ash, the man I still loved. He made an incomprehensible sound. Catching my face between his hands once more, leaning his own face close to mine. His silver eyes had a strange and dazzling sheen to them, and in the very next moment, I realized the cause. Ash, my fierce, implacable vampire lover, was weeping, weeping like an inconsolable child.

That was when I knew the truth: I was going to die.

"Candace," Ash said, as if, by the simple act of repeating my name, he could hold back death, keep me alive. "You've been attacked. You've lost a lot of blood. Too much to stay alive. I can save you. There is a way. But there isn't much time."

I ran my tongue across my lips, summoning up the courage to say the word that was between us. That had always been between us.

"Vampire."

"Yes," Ash said at once. "The only way I can save you is to make you a vampire. The last time we saw each other, we parted in anger. I know you must feel you don't have any reason to trust me. I'm begging you to do it anyhow. Trust me, Candace. Let me save you."

"Ash," I managed. "Don't—"

"*No,*" he said, fiercely, cutting me off. "Do you hear me, Candace? I said, no. Ask anything else you want of me, but don't ask for this. *Do not make me sit here and watch you die.*"

I pulled in what might very well be my last full breath. The pain in my throat was like hot knives.

"Ash . . . ," I said again, desperate to make myself understood this time. I might not have another chance.

"Do not let me go."

I heard him give a sob then, and he brought his lips to mine. But I could barely feel his kiss. Gently, yet swiftly, he lowered me back against the couch. Without taking his eyes from mine, he reached beside him to the low table and brought up a small ivory-handled knife. I had seen it before. The night when he told me what he was. I knew how he would use it now. What must be done.

He opened the blade then set the tip against the inside of his bare arm, bore down. Deeper than he needed to, I think, as if to counterbalance my pain with his own. Bright-red blood welled up at once, streamed down his arm. I heard a clatter as he released the knife back onto the tabletop, and then he was lifting me up once more.

"You understand what has to happen?" he asked. I nodded. I couldn't have spoken even if I had known what to say. "Then drink, my love. Let me save you. Let me save us both."

Gently, he eased my face down, toward where his blood flowed. Willing my mind to ignore the actions of my body, I fastened my lips upon the wound and began to suck. As the taste of blood filled my mouth, began to fill my being, my head jerked back, just once. But Ash was there, gently holding me in place until my resistance gave way to a hunger so elemental it could not be denied.

This was the first step on my journey to becoming what Ash was. The taking of his blood. Then Ash would take mine. He would drink from me until I was no longer alive. Then I would feed again, and the blood I took from him, coursing through my veins, would revive me in my new existence as a vampire.

As he felt me begin to accept, Ash made one last, gutteral sound. Then bent his head, sank his teeth deep into my throat, and finished the job the first vampire had begun.

I surfaced again to a world of red. A world of pain and desire. Blood. My mouth would never lose the taste of it; my body would never lose its craving for it. Ash was holding me away from him now, his silver eyes pinning mine as we faced each other down the length of the couch.

"What do you want, Candace?" he demanded. "Tell me what you want."

I pushed against his hold, struggling to get closer. "You know. You have to know," I panted out.

"I want to hear you say it. I *need* to hear you say it."

"I want you," I all but shouted. "I want your blood. Inside my mouth. Inside my body. Inside my heart. You started this, you sonofabitch. Now let's finish it. Don't think I'm going to let you stop now."

He released me to tear his shirt open with a single yank. The fabric gave way with a high, keening sound. Ash bared his chest. Then, reaching for the knife, pressed it into my hand.

"Take it, Candace," he said. "Take what you need. Take what is already yours."

I surged forward, pushing him back against the padded arm of the couch. I took the tip of the knife and ran it across the width of his naked chest, then plunged the knife into the back of the couch. A line of red welled up where I had drawn the knife. I bent my head, and followed the path of the knife with my tongue. I felt Ash's hands come up to cradle the back of my head, urging me to feed, reveling in my desire for his blood.

"More," he said, his voice husky. "Candace, take more." Without warning, he yanked my head back and to the side. I gave a growl, desperate to feed. Slowly, deliberately, his eyes again on mine, Ash tilted his own head, exposing the long, muscular line of his throat. For several seconds, we regarded one another.

"Take more, Candace," he urged again.

I felt a different kind of hunger flood me then. Not just for Ash's blood, but for Ash himself, for who and what he was; a hunger I was pretty certain had started the very day we'd met, that I knew now would last as long, and longer, than life. I leaned forward, turning his face back toward me, and brought his mouth to mine. I swept my tongue into his mouth, tasted my own blood as he bit down on it, hard. My blood. His blood. It was all the same. All desire.

My mouth left his to run nipping kisses down the length of his neck. I swear I heard him make a sound of pleasure as I sank my teeth into his throat. I fed until my whole world turned red, and I could remember no other color.

When I was aware again, I was on my side, lying quietly in Ash's arms. My head was in his lap, one arm curled beneath his leg, the other extending forward into space. My legs stretched out. I could feel Ash's fingers stroking gently through my hair, and it seemed to me I felt them tremble ever so slightly. No longer dark and indistinct, the world seemed clear and sharp. As if before I'd only seen the world through a filter, and now it had been pulled aside. Everything around me seemed so crisp and clean; even inanimate objects possessed the power to startle the eye. Without moving my head, I gazed around.

My earlier impressions had been correct. I was in an opulent living room, lying on a leather couch. A rosewood coffee table sat just at my eye level. Beneath it, an expanse of honey-colored wood floor streamed out in all directions, till the dark corners of the room swallowed it up. Opposite where I lay, between two windows, with drapes pulled closed, a single lamp with a stained-glass shade cast jeweled patterns on the wall. I had a vague impression of objects crowding together, hugging the edges of the room, just out of range of my vision.

I moved my legs, discovered that they functioned. The second I moved, I felt Ash's fingers pause. I rolled onto my back, face up, and met his eyes. Those strange and wonderful eyes of silver that I'd loved from the moment I first saw him. I couldn't quite read their expression.

"Are you all right?" he asked, quietly.

A laugh rose up, escaped me, before I could help it. Such a prosaic, everyday sort of question. But then, if I'd been the one to speak first, I might very well have said, "Where am I?"

"I'm not quite sure I know," I answered honestly. "I'm thinking it will take a little time to figure out."

"Fair enough," Ash said, but I thought I could hear the way he had to work to keep his voice steady, his emotions under control. I realized then, how taut his body felt as I lay against it. As if stretched almost to the breaking point, it was holding so many different things inside.

"Candace," Ash said. "I . . ."

I reached up then, and pressed the fingers of my right hand against his lips to silence him. And it was only as his own hand came up to capture mine, holding my palm against his face as he closed his eyes and turned to press his lips against the center of my palm, that I realized the pain in my hand was gone. I flexed my fingers, felt Ash's tighten. My whole arm should be screaming in pain. My right wrist should be broken.

Except it wasn't.

I pulled my hand away then, fingers fumbling at my throat, my throat that had been savaged, torn open. It was smooth and whole. I felt a sob rise up then, as inexorable as the laugh had been just moments before.

As a human, I was torn and bleeding.

As a vampire, I was whole.

"Don't," Ash said suddenly, pulling me upright, his arms at my shoulders, supporting me. He pressed a quick, hard kiss against my mouth. My mouth that, just moments ago, I'd used to drink his blood. To make me what he was. "Don't say you regret this, Candace. Don't even think it."

"I don't," I said in a shaky voice. "I'm not. It's just . . ." I began to tremble then, uncontrollably, as I felt the truth come home.

The last time I had seen Ash, I'd felt so furious and betrayed I had come within a hair's breadth of taking him out. But when faced with the choice between a vampire's existence or none at all, I had taken the path Ash offered. The thing I'd fought so long and hard against had finally come true in spite of me. The world looked different because I was different. I was a vampire. And the only constant in a world suddenly turned upside down was Ash himself.

"Hold on to me, Ash," I begged through teeth that had suddenly begun to chatter. "Hold me. Don't let me go."

"Never," he answered, and I felt his arms tighten. "Listen to me, Candace. You are mine forever. I will never let you go."

"Okay," I managed as, to my horror, I struggled against the hot prick of tears at the back of my eyes. I suppose I might have been considered entitled under the circumstances, but the truth is, I seriously hate to cry. It always seems like such a useless thing to do.

"Forever. That sounds about right." The tears came anyway then. There was not a thing on earth I could have done to stop them. "Oh, Jesus, Ash, I thought I was going to die."

"I thought so, too," he said simply, and even through my tears, I heard the horror in his voice. "I thought I was too late—that I did not get to you in time."

"But you did," I said. "You did. You always do. Why is that, I wonder?"

"Don't be stupid, Candace," Ash said mildly, and suddenly I was laughing instead of crying. So much had changed. So much would stay the same. "You know the answer to that as well as I do."

I wiped the tears from my face with the backs of my hands, looked up into those silver eyes.

"That doesn't mean I wouldn't like to hear you say it anyway," I told him. "I haven't changed that much."

"I came for you because I love you, Candace," Ash said, softly. "I will never let you go, because I'll always love you."

"That was the right answer," I said. And brought his mouth to mine.

I felt the passion fill me then, a desire for Ash stronger than any craving for blood. I had done things with Ash I had never imagined I was capable of doing, wanted things with him I had not known it was possible to want. But there had always been one fundamental difference between us, one fundamental barrier: I was a living, breathing human being; Ash was not. But now, as I felt his lips leave mine to roam across my face, as I felt those strong, fierce hands molding my body to his, holding me close, I realized that this last barrier between us was gone. Not quite equal, I was still too newly made for that, and Ash too strong. But no longer different. Now we were the same. Both vampires.

I pushed myself upright, twisted so that I straddled him, then slowly eased him back to lie beneath me on the couch. I could feel his body begin to stir, my own need sharpen, focus. My desire for Ash was like a fever in my blood. I could feel it pouring through my veins. Clean, pure lust. My body was a well-honed tool, every single inch of it ready to do with as I wished. And, in that moment, I thought I understood the truth. The most heady power of the vampire wasn't the ability to control another. It was the knowledge that, finally, at long last, you had been granted the ability to truly control yourself.

I rocked ever so gently, reveling in the slide of my body against the hardening form of Ash's cock. He lay perfectly still, as if content for the moment to watch me enjoying my newfound powers, his eyes as bright as silver coins. The button-down shirt I had worn to the movies had long since been taken off. Beneath it, I wore a tight-fitting undershirt, a lacy bra. I crossed my arms in front of my chest, hooked my thumbs under the edge of the T-shirt, then drew it up and off. Ash didn't make a sound. But his hands came up to caress my skin, slid down to where my body spanned his, my pace slightly more urgent now. I put my hands to the clasp on the front of my bra, slid it open. I shrugged, thrusting my breasts forward even as Ash's hands came up to ease the bra from my shoulders. And then his mouth was there, pulling one breast deep as he reared up. I made a sound at the back of my throat.

Too much, I thought. *Too much*. Too many barriers still between us. Too many clothes. When what I wanted was skin to skin, mouth to mouth, heart to heart, soul to soul. My fingers flew at the buttons on his jeans, desperate to have them off him, even as I felt him lift me to deal with my own. But when he would have turned me to lie beneath him, I resisted.

"No, Ash," I panted. "Let me . . . I want . . ."

"Show me," he said as his fingers danced along my spine. I arched back and felt his mouth at my breast once more. His clever fingers, teasing at my clit.

"Take what you want, Candace. Take me. Take it all."

I pushed him back against the couch, centered myself over him, then, slowly, my eyes never leaving his, I sank down. I saw his lips part, his eyes go from bright and cool to white-hot metal. Blind. I began to rock again, feeling him in the very core of my body, so hard and deep I swear I felt him bump against my heart. I eased up, paused for a fraction of a second, then sank down, once more.

Mine, I thought. *Mine.* Now and forever. No matter what happens. He had saved me, and I would never let him go.

I felt his hands at the notch of my thighs. I lifted one hand, brought it to my lips, pulled one thumb deep inside my mouth. His cock pulsed inside me in answer. My hips were moving of their own accord now. Up and down. Up and down. Ash took his thumb from my mouth and slid it across the head of my clit. I cried out. Every cell in my body was screaming at me to go fast, go faster. Ruthlessly, I held it down. Forcing myself to a slow and steady rhythm, inexorable as waves against the shore. Holding my passion back, feeling it pound like the heartbeat I no longer possessed, making my body pulse and throb. And Ash was moving with me. Thrusting up to meet me, his hands like fire across my bare skin.

"Come for me," I panted. "Let me watch you, Ash. I want to see you fly."

"I have wings for that," he managed, and made me laugh, and as I did I felt my passion slip its bonds.

"I know. Oh, damn it anyway. Oh, *God.*"

I heard him laugh then, the sound so filled with joy.

"Together. Together, Candace. Now and forever."

I felt his arms wrap around me. I held on tight. Together, we flung ourselves out over the void.

Three

"Wings," I said, some time later. Ash and I were lying entwined on the couch. "Wings. That's what it was."

"What *what* was?" Ash inquired.

Now that our lovemaking was over, he'd pulled a soft blanket around my shoulders for warmth. The truth was, my bodily sensations sort of faded in and out. One moment, everything was sharp and focused, the next, indistinct. It was as if my body was still tuning in to its own personal wavelength as a vampire. What it felt like to be human, what it meant to be a vampire, were all jumbled up inside me. I couldn't quite make the two join.

"Right before the attack," I said. I thought for a moment, casting my mind back. "I heard a sound I thought I recognized. But it was over so quickly, the attack was so sudden, I didn't have the chance to figure out what it was at the time. I think it was wings, the wings of the vampire."

Ash was silent for a moment, rubbing the palm

of one hand absently back and forth over my shoulder.

"Did you see who it was?"

I frowned. "Sort of. Just bits and pieces, really, it all happened so fast. He was a Hollywood vampire."

Ash's hand stopped moving. "What?"

"You know—a Hollywood vampire," I said. "Obvious. Dark hair. Dark eyes."

"I see," Ash said, and I thought I heard the faintest edge of laughter in his voice. It made me happy to realize I could make him laugh even in these extreme circumstances. It made me feel the world might yet right itself, somehow. "Hollywood vampire, hmmm," Ash went on. "Dare I ask if I have a type?"

I settled my head a little more firmly onto his knee. "Absolutely," I said. "They call it: one of a kind."

He leaned down, dropped a kiss on the top of my head.

"I'm pretty sure I marked him," I went on, after a moment. "I caught him with silver down one side of his face. Not enough to take him out, just enough to make him let go. I'm sure he now has a nice long scar."

"I'm glad to hear it," Ash said. "It will make him

easier to recognize if he's stupid enough to stick around."

Ash will hunt that vampire down, I thought. I had been threatened once, several months ago, attacked by a group of street thugs. Ash had found and killed the man responsible for setting up the attack twelve hours after I told him about it.

I sat up. "So what happens now?"

"What do you want to happen?" Ash asked in a carefully neutral voice.

I felt my first spurt of annoyance. I shifted myself off Ash's lap, scooting to the far end of the couch. I kept the blanket. Apparently, I was still human enough to equate being naked with being vulnerable.

"I'm serious, Ash," I said. "I want to know."

"What makes you think I'm not serious?" he asked at once. "It's not a simple question, Candace. You don't have the same boundaries you used to. That means you don't have the same possibilities for what happens next, either."

"All right. I guess I can buy that," I acknowledged. "It still doesn't tell me what I need to know. I have a life, Ash, or I had one. I'm not so sure I do anymore. I'm not so sure I know who I am."

"Becoming a vampire doesn't change the fundamentals of who you are," Ash replied. "You are who you have always been, Candace. You're also something more."

"A bloodsucker," I said, unable to keep the bitterness from my tone. Now that the initial fear of death, the initial joy at the fact that I survived at all were beginning to dim, I could see the reality that the crisis had pushed to the background.

Maybe Ash is right, I thought. Becoming a vampire hadn't changed me in the ways that counted most. Because I still had the same problem I had always had. The thought of surviving on the blood of living things filled me with revulsion.

"I don't want this," I whispered, the words welling up and out before I could stop them. "I never wanted it, no matter how much I wanted you. I don't want to kill people and take their blood!" I dropped my head down into my hands. "Sweet Jesus, what have I let you do to me? What have I done?"

"The only thing you could," Ash answered simply, but his tone was firm as iron. "And you haven't taken living blood, Candace. You've only taken mine. As long as you feed only on me, your transition is incomplete. I gave you that much."

I lifted my head. "I don't think I understand. Gave me what?"

"A choice," Ash said. "You are not yet irrevocably a vampire. That comes only with your first taste of living blood. But I can only sustain you for so long. And the longer you resist completing the transition, the stronger your bloodlust will become.

"Make no mistake, Candace," Ash continued. "I want you in my world with me, fully a vampire. It's what I've always wanted. But of your own free will, not by force."

"But all you're really saying is that my options are the same as they've always been," I said, unable to keep the dismay out of my voice. "Become a vampire—a true vampire—or die. The only difference I can see between making this decision yesterday and making it today is that now I won't make it as a human, I'll make it as a vampire."

"But that makes all the difference, don't you see?"

"No," I said. "I'm sorry, but I don't. It's impossible, Ash. It always has been."

"Only because you refuse to see it any other way."

I would have stood then, but Ash was too quick for me. He reached out to catch me by my upper arms.

"Let me go."

"No," Ash said. "I want you to listen to me, Candace. You're doing the same thing you did when you were human. The same thing you've always done. You're closing your mind, your heart, to possibilities. You want to walk away from me? Go on, try it."

I did my best to jerk away, but Ash's grip only tightened.

"I'm not going to let you do it, Candace," he said, an intensity in his voice greater than any I had ever heard there before. "*I will not let you go.* If I was willing to do that, you would be dead by now.

"Why can't you learn to see with new eyes? Look at what's happened as a gift. Stop fighting and reach for me as I reach for you. Reach out and hold on."

I stared at him, forgetting to struggle in sheer astonishment. "A gift," I said. "Are you out of your mind?"

Ash hauled me forward then, until his face was just inches from mine. His eyes burned bright enough to light the whole world.

"I love you, Candace. I've loved you from the very first moment I saw you. Do you love me?"

"What does that have to do with—"

He gave me a quick shake, cutting me off. "Just answer the question," he said. "Do you love me? Yes or no?"

"Yes, damn you," I said. "You know I do. Satisfied now?"

"Not by a long shot," Ash said, but he smiled

and dropped a hard, swift kiss on my mouth. "Start thinking like a woman in love, Candace. A whole new world is opening before you, and all you can do is react like a little girl afraid of the dark."

"But I *am* afraid of the dark," I said. "Can't you see that's the problem? It's dark and I'm scared and I don't know which way to go. There's more to a relationship than just spectacular sex, Ash. There's even more than love."

"I know that, Candace," Ash said simply. His arms gentled around me then. I leaned into him, rested my head against his chest. "I know. And I know what I've asked of you, joining me in my world, has seemed unthinkable. But the unthinkable became reality about two hours ago."

He shifted back to gaze down into my face, caressing it with a featherlight touch.

"Can you really not see the way everything has changed?" he asked. "I've seen our future . . . in my world. All you've been able to see is the unknown. But now you can decide whether or not to be with me as one of us. You're not an outsider anymore, Candace. *You are a vampire.*

"If I'd been even two minutes later, we wouldn't be having this conversation. You'd be dead. But you're not. And now we have a chance to be together. A chance we never could have predicted or looked for. We *have* been given a gift. The gift of time. But if you waste it, if you fight what's happened, it will slip away. We'll both be left with nothing."

I opened my mouth then closed it again. "That's quite a speech," I said.

"Yes, but has it convinced you?" Ash answered with the glimmer of a smile. It faded as quickly as it had flickered into being, and he was serious once more.

"The way I see it, things are really very simple, Candace. We love each other. We deserve a chance to be together. We have that chance now. I say we take it with both hands, hold on to it for as long as we can make it last."

These were the kinds of words a woman dreams of hearing from the man she loves, I thought. *If Ash and I were human, would I be hesitating as I am now?*

Of course not, I realized. I'd be seizing the chance he spoke of with both hands. Grabbing hold of my own happiness and holding it as if I'd never let it go. The truly unnatural element in the situation was me. I was the one willing to throw away our chance for love.

"You're right," I said slowly. "Being afraid of the dark doesn't have to make me blind."

I felt a tremor run through him. Felt the power

of my love, my choice. I reached up, and brought his lips down to mine.

"Love me, Ash," I murmured as his mouth left mine to press fierce kisses across my face. "Love me like there's no tomorrow."

His lips found mine again, captured them in a searing kiss. "You're getting it backward," he said. "There are more tomorrows than you can count."

And then, again, we were making love.

Four

"The thing you have to remember," Ash said as we walked through the luxurious hallway that linked the Beijing's residential wing with its casino, "is that most of what humans feel and think is utterly trivial, even to them. There's no reason for you to consider it at all. But there is a knack to learning how to filter the wave of information humans put out. A knack that takes practice. That's why we're here tonight."

The end of the hallway opened into the casino, and we were greeted with a wave of sound. Was the Sher, the casino where I worked, this loud and I no longer noticed? Another sound pierced the casino's cacophony. My cell phone, completely forgotten since the attack, was ringing in my purse. I pulled it out, stared at it as if I had never seen such an object.

"Who is it?" Ash asked.

"Bibi," I said, seeing her name on the screen.

Bibi Schwartz was my best friend, one of the few humans who knew about vampires, and the only person I'd told about Ash. We hadn't talked in two days. She was undoubtedly wondering where I was. "I can't talk to her now," I said, still staring at the phone. I couldn't tell Bibi what had happened. I couldn't deal with her at all.

Ash lifted the phone from my hand, slipped it back in my purse. "You'll talk with her later," he said. "Now there are things you must learn."

Ash and I had spent the last two days together, all of it in the privacy of his apartment. Somehow it didn't occur to me to return to my own house. The woman who lived there didn't exist anymore—and it was almost as if the house didn't, either. So we stayed together, at Ash's, exploring my newly acquired vampire powers. Not that mine were anywhere near as developed as Ash's, of course. The aspect of my new existence that was strongest was still what I'd noticed first. The world literally looked different, leaner—clearer, more in focus. My other senses had expanded as well. Taste, touch, smell. It was as if I'd gone from tube technology to HDTV. Every single experience was heightened.

Satisfied that I was now reasonably comfortable in my new vampire skin, Ash had decided it was time to take my period of adjustment to the next level: exploring the capacity of my new vampire mind. Step one: direct human interaction. So we had returned to the Strip, to the Beijing, the most luxurious of the new casinos, where Ash happened to have a penthouse condo.

"What I'm going to ask you to do is a matter of focus," Ash explained.

"And here I thought you were taking me out." I took a few more steps past one of the blackjack tables, when somewhat to my surprise, my feet slowed. *What's this about?* I wondered.

I was enthusiastic about the evening's adventure. I had visited vampire hangouts while still human. All I was doing now was turning the tables, and it wasn't as if a casino setting was unfamiliar. I did work in one, after all. But the farther I moved into the casino, the more overwhelming the wave of sensory information became.

"I *am* taking you out," Ash replied. "We're just doing some multitasking along the way. It's something we vampires are very good at."

"You are so romantic."

"And you're stalling, Candace." He put firm but gentle fingers in the center of my back. "Come on. Let's go."

With Ash propelling me, we made a slow circuit of the casino floor. More than once I was grateful for the pressure of his fingers at my back. Without them, I might have simply stopped, cold. *Blood.* I could hear it, rushing through thousands of human veins; hear the beating of hundreds of human hearts. Sweat dripping down a nervous bettor's cheek sounded like a spring creek in full flood. Fingertips drumming nervously on a denim-clad knee were as loud as gunshots.

I turned my head to look up at Ash. "Are things always this loud?"

"Initially, yes," Ash replied. "That's one of the reasons I wanted us to come out tonight. The trick is to let the human sensory input flow over you, through you. Don't let it lead or distract. You choose when to get involved. The ability to choose is the first step to gaining control—over them and yourself."

All of a sudden I gave a quick shiver. I knew what he meant—this was establishing rapport. Among other things, it was how vampires who fed on humans selected their victims, then made them submissive, bending them to their will before delivering the coup de grâce. Rapport was something I had always considered nearly as revolting as having your throat torn open.

"Let's try an experiment," Ash suggested. He nodded toward a man sitting not far off, at the end of a row of slot machines. "What can you tell me about him?"

I looked, considered for a moment. Some things were obvious, even without my vampire abilities.

"He's getting older, for one," I replied. "I'd put him mid- to late sixties, probably from a rural background."

"What makes you say that?" Ash asked.

"His clothes. Worn denim, snap-front shirt. And those cowboy boots are not for show." I cocked my head, narrowed my eyes as if drawing a bead on him. "You see the way he's sitting? His back hurts. It has for a long time."

"So far, so good," Ash said. "But not really anything the guy sitting next to him couldn't see just as well. Who *is* that old man, Candace? What can you tell me that takes *our* eyes?"

I gazed at the old man, letting everything else fall away, narrowing my focus to him the same way I'd just narrowed my eyes. For several moments, nothing seemed to happen. *What if I can't do this?* I thought. *Were my senses less acute, diminished because I hadn't fed on living blood?* Then, with a suddenness that left me dizzy, all my vampire senses seemed to snap into play at once. I was inside the old man's skin, inside his head, though I wouldn't have called what I was experiencing reading his mind. I didn't hear complete sentences, specific thoughts. It was more like a series of still images in rapid succession, a flip-book of his life.

His face, as it was now, superimposed on what it had been years ago. *He was once a handsome man,* I thought in some surprise. I saw children, a woman in an apron standing in a dingy kitchen with an old-fashioned linoleum floor. And then an image of the man himself, head down on his arms at the table, sobbing as if his heart would break, and I understood in that moment what the trip to Vegas was all about. To forget. To use the bright lights and loud noises to block out the fact that the house was empty now. His wife, dead. His children, gone.

"Now reach back, Candace," I heard Ash say.

I pulled my senses back, reaching deep inside myself, until I found the place that was still and silent, that had no living counterpart. *The undead place,* I thought. And I drew that place up and out until it filled my body, filled my mind. *This is who I am now.* This was my center, my place of control. The place I must inhabit in order to survive. And, in that moment, I understood the essence of establishing rapport. It was establishing this balance. To see the human needs, but to respond as something other than human. I could still see the old man's pain, read it as clearly as print on a page, but it no longer had the power to touch me. I was undead, isolated, a being apart.

I was a vampire.

"He's desperate," I heard myself say, my voice absolutely calm. "Everyone he loves is gone. He'll *do* something desperate before very much longer."

Even as we watched, the old man seemed to explode. Screaming at the slot machine, pounding it with both hands. Security appeared in the blink of an eye. Flanking him on either side, jerking him from his seat. He fought like a cornered dog.

"He thinks he's got nothing left to lose," I said. I pulled all my senses back then, into myself. "He's about to discover that he's wrong."

"You did well," Ash said as we watched the casino's security hustle the old man from the floor. "You learn fast, but then I expected as much."

"Then why don't I like myself very much?"

"Because you understand his pain and wish you could stop it," Ash said simply. "Because, in spite of what your vampire's mind knows, you're still reacting with a human's emotions. I didn't say this would be easy, Candace. Only that it was necessary. And you did do well. You stayed in control. That's important, particularly for you."

I didn't need to ask what he meant. I knew well enough. If I couldn't learn to control myself, I would eventually give in to the desire that would make me a vampire forever: the desire to drink living blood. My new abilities were a double-edged sword. They made humans easier to fathom, to direct or misdirect. They also made them impossible to ignore.

Blood, I thought once more.

It was all around me, whispering in my ear, stroking all my senses, tantalizing . . . arousing. The feelings it evoked made me want to run in the opposite direction, even as they inspired me to come back for more. All of a sudden, I had a whole new perspective on the vampires I used to eject from the Scheherazade. It wasn't just the thrill of getting the better of humans that made them spend so much time trying to cheat the casinos. It was the thrill of human attention itself.

"What's next?" I asked.

"Since you passed the test, we get to celebrate."

"Celebrate? I just violated that man's mind and memories."

"Perhaps. But you also learned what you're going to need to survive," Ash said. "And you surviving means we can be together. I think that's reason to celebrate. You get to choose. Anything at all."

Ash's silver eyes held me, in them the promise of

pleasures I hadn't even begun to imagine. My discomfort slipped away. I grinned, suddenly knowing exactly what I wanted.

"Follow me and you'll find out."

"That's nice," Ash said agreeably, about an hour later. He was sitting in an overstuffed chair in one of the Beijing's designer boutiques while I modeled what could only be described as evening gowns. This was the fourth so far, and Ash had stated his intention of buying every single one. He took a sip of champagne from the thin flute that rested on an elegant table by his elbow, then made a circular motion with one finger, the ancient male symbol for *turn around and let me see the back*. I was more than happy to oblige.

The dress I'd saved for last was a sheath of rose-colored silk, smooth as honey against my skin, the color a perfect foil for my brown hair and eyes. Scooping my hair up from my neck, I made a slow pivot, glancing back at Ash over my shoulder as I turned around and watched his eyes go wide. From the front, the dress was simple, almost demure, with a ballet-style neckline. But the back was pure temptation. Plunging straight down in a slim *V* that stopped just short of begging the question of whether or not I had on any underwear. It was the sort of dress every woman dreams of owning: one that would make every single man in any room she enters look twice, coming and going.

"Well?" I said as I completed my turn.

Ash's eyes were dancing with mischief. He cocked his head to one side. "Do you know," he said, his tone mild and conversational, "I suddenly discovered that I can't quite make up my mind about this one after all. I think it's because you're too far away. Why don't you come a little closer?"

I took a few steps forward, closing half the distance to where Ash sat.

"How's this?" I inquired.

"Better," Ash said, his tone agreeable. "But not quite close enough."

Slowly, aware of his eyes on me every step of the way, I stepped toward him until we were no more than an arm's length apart. Ash reached out, his fingers tangling with mine, and tugged me down into his lap, his free hand cupping my ass, then sliding upward until his fingers caressed the bare skin of my back. I felt my nipples harden against the soft silk, a tug of pure desire deep in my groin.

"You look thirsty," Ash commented. "I'll bet trying on all those dresses is hard work."

He reached for the champagne flute, held it to my lips, his eyes never leaving mine. The hand that had slid up my back now supported my head as Ash eased it back. I took a sip of champagne, savoring the liquid punch of bubbles down the back of my throat. Ash drew the glass away, then dipped his head and ran his tongue across my lips as if to catch any stray drops.

"Ash," I murmured, even as he slipped his tongue inside my mouth. I caught it between my teeth, bit down, hard, then released. "We're in public."

"So?" He ran a series of nibbling kisses across my cheek, down the side of my neck.

"We'll take this one, too," he said, raising his voice.

"Thank you, sir," said the saleswoman, stepping into view. "An excellent choice."

"Ash," I said, my tone somewhere between exasperation and delight. "Much as my inner diva thanks you, I do feel obliged to point out that I don't have anywhere to wear this dress, let alone the three others you've already agreed to buy."

"You don't know that," Ash said, his tone reasonable. The hand at my back slipped under the silk of the dress at my waist. "For instance, there's tomorrow night."

"What's tomorrow night?"

His hand began to wander now, fingers gently yet persistently inching upward toward my breast. I leaned down, and captured the closest of his earlobes between my teeth, applying pressure until I heard him hiss out a sound before I let it go.

I leaned against him, pressing my breasts against his chest. "You really like this dress?"

"I really like that dress."

"Then tell me about where I'll be wearing it tomorrow night."

"There's an auction I need to attend," Ash explained as his fingers danced along my bare spine. "Very exclusive, invitation only. One of Vegas's premiere collectors died not long ago, and it seems he was the only antiquity his grieving widow was interested in keeping around."

"Don't tell me," I said. "The grieving widow is young."

"Young enough to be foolish and greedy," Ash said. His hand was on the silk now. Gliding gently down the curve of my ass, then sliding around toward the front, the notch between my thighs. "Fortunately, her husband's collection is truly unique. I'm sure the bidding will be quite spirited."

"That ought to perk the grieving widow right up," I remarked. Ash's fingers caressed my belly then began to move upward as he bent his head and ran the tip of his tongue down the length of my throat. I arched against him, savoring the variety of sensations against my skin.

"I've never been to a private auction before," I managed to get out.

"Then it's high time you went to one," Ash said.

His mouth found mine just as his hand reached my breast. Pushing gently upward with the palm of his hand, he ran his thumb back and forth across my nipple. I had a sudden vision of his mouth there, pulling the nipple deep inside.

"Candace," Ash whispered in my ear.

"What?"

"I'm not so sure I should buy you this dress after all. Every man who sees you in it is going to spend way too much time trying to figure out how to get you out of it."

I crossed my legs, feeling the pressure of my body increasing my own pleasure.

"That's precisely why you should buy it," I proposed. "While the other guys are looking at me, you can outbid them and they won't even notice."

I turned my head then, till our lips were no more than a whisper apart.

"I want you, Ash," I said. "I want you right now. Tell me I can have you."

The hand on my breast tightened, fingers squeezing the nipple, and I felt a white-hot stab of desire.

I closed the gap between our lips, urging his open, stroking the inside of his mouth urgently with my tongue. I felt a shudder pass through him as I slid from his lap. Head leaning back, he watched me, the silver of his eyes as bright as sun on water.

"I'll meet you at the elevator to the penthouse." I stood up. The dress slid against me like the promise of sin. "Don't make me wait."

"I'd say you can cross that worry right off the list," Ash said.

I was laughing as I headed back toward the dressing rooms, even as I felt my knees begin to wobble. Wanting Ash was like a shot of whiskey straight to my head. I heard him, speaking to the saleswoman. By the time she joined me in the dressing room, I had managed to get my fingers to stop trembling.

"Sorry about the show," I said as she deftly helped me ease the dress over my head.

She slid it onto a hanger and gave a quick chuckle. "Oh, please. This is Vegas, honey. I really hate to break it to you, but you guys actually looked pretty tame compared to some things I've seen." I saw her throw me a quick, considering glance in the mirror as I pulled on my clothes.

"Everything's taken care of. Mr. Donahue has arranged for us to send your purchases directly to his penthouse."

She slid open the curtain of the dressing room, held it for me as I walked out.

"Thanks—"

"Julie," she said.

"Thanks, Julie. "I wonder, could you tell me . . ."

"Of course I can," she interrupted with a smile. "Lingerie is right around the corner."

Fifteen minutes later I had exactly what I wanted. A sinful leotard made entirely of lace, open at the crotch. Another woman might have chosen something red or black. I had opted for an icy, virginal white. In keeping with the color, the neckline was high, particularly by Vegas standards, plunging no lower than my collarbones. To offset this, a slit ran down the very center, leaving the inner outline of my breasts exposed. The lace swirled around my body in a pattern of curving, twisting flowers and vines that reached up to my breasts like teasing fingers, stopping just short of the nipples, as if they were the goal. I could see them through the pattern, like dusky blossoms. At my crotch a rose bloomed.

I looked at myself in the mirror, discovered I was grinning. I looked like an eager, slightly naughty bride who knew precisely what the upcoming night held in store. Slowly, the smile faded as I realized the truth. I *felt* like a bride. Ash and I were beginning a whole new existence together, an existence which, once I had decided to embrace it at all, I had embraced with all my being, all my heart. From the moment I had agreed to give joining Ash in his world a genuine chance, I had barely looked back.

Who are you, Candace? I suddenly thought. *Do you still know?* What kind of person was I that I could turn my back on everyone and everything I loved in the world of living without so much as a backward glance?

But I'm not a person, I thought. *Not like they are. Not anymore. That's precisely what joining Ash in his world means. I'm not human. I am a vampire.*

As if the acknowledgment had summoned up some new level of change, of commitment, my reflection in the mirror abruptly winked out. With a cry of horror, I lurched forward, my knuckles rapping against the mirror so hard it cracked. With a second cry, I staggered back. The sight of that cracked and empty mirror was almost more than I could bear.

"Ma'am," I heard the shop attendant's alarmed voice say. She knocked briskly on the door. "Do you need assistance? Is everything all right?"

Somehow I found my voice. "It's fine," I said, my eyes riveted to the glass. The crack in the mirror spread across it like a spiderweb, but it reflected back nothing, nothing at all.

"Is there anything else I can bring you?" she asked.

I sat down on the padded bench in the dressing room, fighting against a sudden, hysterical urge. I wasn't quite certain whether it was to laugh or cry.

"No, thank you," I said, my voice sounding strange even to my own ears. "I'll be right out."

"Take your time."

I dropped my face down into my hands. *Time. The commodity I can never get enough of.*

Stop it, Candace! I suddenly thought. *You made this choice. Stop feeling sorry for yourself. Go after what you want.*

And what I truly wanted tonight was the fulfillment of all the things with which the evening had begun. The thrill of new experiences. The special anticipation that only comes when love and lust combine. I wanted this night of Ash and I together in two worlds at once.

And I'm going to have it, I thought. Filled with fresh determination, I stood up, quickly put my street clothes on over the leotard. Nothing was going to stop this night from happening—or prevent me from fulfilling my own desires, and those of the man I loved.

I would fight for my time with Ash, however long it lasted, with all the strength I had. Even if the greatest foe I faced was myself.

Five

I spotted Ash standing in the elegant circular lobby of the Beijing's residential tower. He stood near one of the elevators, a bas relief Chinese landscape on the wall behind him. Arms folded loosely across his chest, legs slightly spread with the weight on the balls of his feet, as if ready to move in any direction at a moment's notice. His expression was neutral, perfectly pleasant, but utterly unreadable. His silver eyes catching the light of the brass chandelier above, without once revealing his thoughts. I let my footsteps slow, then stop altogether.

When was the last time I did this? I suddenly wondered. Had I ever done it? Watched Ash without his realizing it. With the exception of the night we met, when I literally spotted him across a crowded room, I simply could not remember a time when I had gazed at Ash and did not find him there before me, already gazing back. Our relationship wasn't a game, but a series of moves and counter-moves nevertheless, with Ash always one step ahead.

The pose he assumed now appeared casual, but it came to me as I stood looking at him that there was absolutely nothing casual about Ash. Nothing wasted, even in repose. With all his energy in reserve, his form seemed clearer, more distinct than those of the humans flowing around him. Humans waste energy, expending it in a thousand different directions. Ash was star-bright, diamond-hard.

I took a step toward him then stopped short, as a flash of movement on the far side of the lobby caught my eye. Just for a second, I could have sworn I saw a dark-haired man gazing at Ash as intently as I was. Down the right side of his face, he bore a scar.

"Ash!" I said suddenly, starting forward, my tone alarmed. He moved toward me instantly.

"What is it, Candace? What's wrong?"

By the time I reached him, the dark-haired man was gone. Vanishing so completely that I was almost convinced he'd never been there at all. Apparently my eyes were still playing tricks.

"It's nothing," I said. "I thought I saw something, that's all. But it isn't there now."

I reached for him then, linked my arms around

his neck, and drew him close, felt the
of need deep in my gut.

"Take me upstairs, Ash," I said. "Tak   upstairs and make the world go away."

"I can do that," he said.

And I believed him, with all my heart.

We stepped into the elevator. We were the only
ones in it and, instinctively, each of us took opposite
sides of the car. Ash slid a key card in for the penthouse, then his hand paused and he lifted his silver
eyes to mine. That was the moment it hit me: The
last time I stepped into an elevator with Ash I had
been human, and I almost hadn't made it out alive.

Abruptly, I realized my hand had risen to my
throat, as if to protect it, in an action I performed
entirely without conscious thought. Images, sensations, crowded for possession of my body and
mind. Pain. Fear. Blood. Ash kept his gaze steady
on mine. From across the elevator, I could see my
own memories of the most terrible moment of our
past reflected in his eyes.

No! I thought. *That's not what I want!*

Because there had been other things in that long-
ago elevator as well, things I had buried deep in
order to stay sane and survive. The reasons for getting into it in the first place: Passion. Desire. Love.

Slowly, my muscles as stiff as if they had been clenched for hours, I slid my hand down from my throat. I felt my fingers brush against my own shirt collar, drop to the top button. And, quite suddenly, I knew what it was I wanted. I could not erase the memory of that first, terrible night. It would be with me, always. But I could supplant it with something else.

This, I thought as, my eyes on Ash's, I eased the top shirt button open. *I choose this. This is what I want.*

I let my fingers roam a little farther, fingertips sliding across the lace of the leotard I'd hidden beneath my street clothes, until they reached the second shirt button to ease it open as well. As it popped free of the buttonhole, I saw the passion flare in Ash's eyes. A sudden, vivid flash of heat swept through my body. I could have sworn I felt Ash's fingers at my breasts, stroking the nipples to stiff, needy points. The heat plunged, straight down between my thighs. My clit began to pulse and throb. From across the elevator, I could see Ash's eyes begin to shine with passion, knew what I saw there was the mirror of what was in my own.

Rapport, I thought, the vampire's special power. I would use it now. I could make my lover's blood race without a single touch. With no more than a his neck, and drew him close, felt the hard punch of need deep in my gut.

"Take me upstairs, Ash," I said. "Take me upstairs and make the world go away."

"I can do that," he said.

And I believed him, with all my heart.

We stepped into the elevator. We were the only ones in it and, instinctively, each of us took opposite sides of the car. Ash slid a key card in for the penthouse, then his hand paused and he lifted his silver eyes to mine. That was the moment it hit me: The last time I stepped into an elevator with Ash I had been human, and I almost hadn't made it out alive.

Abruptly, I realized my hand had risen to my throat, as if to protect it, in an action I performed entirely without conscious thought. Images, sensations, crowded for possession of my body and mind. Pain. Fear. Blood. Ash kept his gaze steady on mine. From across the elevator, I could see my own memories of the most terrible moment of our past reflected in his eyes.

No! I thought. *That's not what I want!*

Because there had been other things in that long-ago elevator as well, things I had buried deep in order to stay sane and survive. The reasons for getting into it in the first place: Passion. Desire. Love.

Slowly, my muscles as stiff as if they had been clenched for hours, I slid my hand down from my throat. I felt my fingers brush against my own shirt collar, drop to the top button. And, quite suddenly, I knew what it was I wanted. I could not erase the memory of that first, terrible night. It would be with me, always. But I could supplant it with something else.

This, I thought as, my eyes on Ash's, I eased the top shirt button open. *I choose this. This is what I want.*

I let my fingers roam a little farther, fingertips sliding across the lace of the leotard I'd hidden beneath my street clothes, until they reached the second shirt button to ease it open as well. As it popped free of the buttonhole, I saw the passion flare in Ash's eyes. A sudden, vivid flash of heat swept through my body. I could have sworn I felt Ash's fingers at my breasts, stroking the nipples to stiff, needy points. The heat plunged, straight down between my thighs. My clit began to pulse and throb. From across the elevator, I could see Ash's eyes begin to shine with passion, knew what I saw there was the mirror of what was in my own.

Rapport, I thought, the vampire's special power. I would use it now. I could make my lover's blood race without a single touch. With no more than a wish, he could respond. *You want to play? Okay, let's play, Ash,* I thought, and saw his lips curve into a smile.

Keeping my eyes on his, I deliberately shifted my stance, parting my legs, pushing my pelvis forward as I pressed my shoulders back against the elevator wall. At once I felt his presence there, phantom fingers pressing, sliding, stroking. From across the elevator, I could see the way his cock made a solid ridge against the front of his pants. *My turn, now,* I thought. I was smiling as I closed my eyes, the better to conjure up the image of my desire in my mind.

Ash with his head thrown back and me on my knees before him. My hands strongly kneading the taut muscles of his butt. Embracing his body, cradling the length of his erection between my breasts, then slowly shifting to brush my stiffened nipples back and forth across it. I could feel his muscles bunch beneath my hands as his pelvis jerked forward; feel his fingers tangle in my hair. I knew what, in his urgency, he wanted. Recognized it for my own desire.

The elevator gave a sudden chime, and my eyes flew open. Ash's face was stark with passion. The doors slid apart. I didn't move. Ash stepped forward, pivoted, then stepped out, moving not toward the dramatic wall of glass that looked out over the Strip but toward the bedroom.

I followed him through the vast rooms, passing low couches and tables, and Egyptian and Greek carvings, each on its own spot-lit pedestal. Ash paused for a moment, touching a dimmer switch that brought a soft glow to the inner rooms. I paused, too, struck once more by how arousing simply watching Ash was. As if to tease me, he picked up his pace. As if to tease him, I let mine slow.

Ahead of me, Ash slid open the bedroom door and a sweet and familiar smell filled the air. Sweet peas. My favorite flower. I could see bouquets of them in the room and petals on the bed. Ash stepped through the bedroom door, and then I was running.

I burst through the doorway, moving at full speed. Ash was waiting for me. I leaped, and he caught me, spinning us around as he let the force of my momentum carry us into the center of the room. I wrapped my legs around his waist, my mouth fused to his, hands streaking over his body. He took four staggering steps back and collapsed backward onto the bed, still holding me tightly. I released his mouth to give a laugh of pure exhilaration, reared back, and tore his shirt open.

"That was my favorite shirt," he protested.

I laughed again, power and desire screaming through my veins, then leaned down to flick my tongue across his nipples. First the right then the left, lapping like a cat at a bowl of cream. They stiffened and I teased them gently with my teeth. Ash gave a groan.

"I'll buy you another one," I promised.

I felt his hands move restlessly across my back, mold themselves to the curves of my ass. "You have on too many clothes."

I pressed a series of kisses up along his jaw until I reached one ear. "Then do something about it."

Ash slipped his hands into the front waistband of my jeans, then moved them downward to slide the buttons from their holes. His fingers lingered for a moment, pressing hard against my clit before he lifted me, drawing the denim down my legs in one slow and easy motion. No sooner had he settled me down again than his hands were fisting in the back of my shirt. With one quick yank, he ripped it open.

"Copycat," I said.

"You'd like to think so." Beneath the torn shirt, his hands moved to the front of my body to my breasts. I thrust them forward, into his caress. "Candace, lift up your arms."

Slowly, I lifted my arms above my head as Ash slid the shirt up my arms and off. Before I could move, he captured my wrists lightly with one hand, holding them in place. I watched as his eyes took in the lace I'd concealed beneath the shirt, saw the way they darkened.

"Well, now," he said, the pleasure like a strain of music in his voice. "This is a nice surprise."

"I was hoping you'd think so."

He shifted then, leaning up, and I felt his tongue slide along my bare skin through the slit in the lace at the front. My stomach muscles began to quiver. Ash turned his head, circled the closest nipple with his tongue, then drew it deep into his mouth. I arched toward his touch, twisting my wrists to break his grasp. Instead, it only tightened. Ash's mouth pulled at my breast as if he could find sustenance there, his tongue flicking wildly back and forth. I cried out.

He released my arms then and lay back, pulling me down with him. Suddenly ravenous, I nipped at his lips, parted them with my tongue, then took Ash's own tongue inside my mouth to suck. With one hand, he held the back of my neck steady. I felt the fingers of the other dance down the length of my spine. They teased the cleft in my butt then slid forward to find the place where the leotard was open at the crotch. As his fingers brushed against my sensitive skin, I jerked, and felt his fingers slip inside me. I tightened around them and began to rock as Ash slowly slid them in and out.

"More," I gasped as I tore my mouth from his. "More, Ash. I'm so hungry for you."

His eyes on mine, he put the pad of the thumb of his free hand to my mouth. I bit down, tasted blood, then pulled it deep inside my mouth, dancing my tongue across it until all trace and taste of blood were gone. Ash drew it out. In the next moment, I felt the slick warmth of it circle against my clit even as his fingers drove into me, hard. With a cry, I pitched forward, pelvis tilted up, hands bracketing Ash's head as it lay against the comforter. His hands increased their tempo, stroking, driving me on.

"How hungry are you, Candace?" he whispered. "Tell me how hungry. Tell me what you want."

"Everything," I said, then gave a groan of sheer ecstasy as he reared up to pull one breast inside his mouth. "Everything, Ash," I panted. "Body. Heart. Mind. Blood."

I felt his teeth scrape against my nipple, then part to surround it as his tongue played back and forth. I quivered, teetering on the breaking point of passion, the world narrowing down to the feel of Ash's hands and mouth. In every act of desire, this moment arrives. The moment when going back becomes impossible. So impossible it no longer even exists. There is only forward. There is only desire's fulfillment, and then, finally, its demise.

The grip of Ash's teeth tightened suddenly. My vision hazed red as I felt a spear of hot pleasure shoot from breast to groin.

"Take it, Candace," he said. "Take what you want."

My body quivering, reaching for the brink, I bent my head and put my teeth to his throat. Then, for a split second, I hesitated. "Take it, Candace," I heard Ash say once more. And felt the slide of his muscle, the taste of his skin inside my mouth.

I bit down, and the whole world exploded.

Ash's blood, inside my mouth. Ash's fingers, inside my body. The pleasure of both so intense that I was gone. I was no longer in the world in any way that I had ever known. Nothing existed except what Ash and I did together. What we created and made together. We were one blood. One love. Desire without end.

"Hold on, Candace," I swore I heard Ash's voice say. "Don't let go."

I won't, I thought. I vowed. *I'll never let you go, Ash. I'll never want to.*

I heard him make a sound then. And knew that it was one of joy.

I woke at dawn. Lifting my head from the pillow to find the room around me just beginning to brighten. Beside me, Ash was still and silent, his own eyes closed. We had made love all night, the curtains of the room pulled back to the lights of the city below us, the light of the stars and moon above. Apparently, we had forgotten to close them.

Driven by some sudden restlessness, a need I could not quite name, I slipped from between the sheets, pulled one of Ash's soft wool robes from the wardrobe, and moved to stand at the window.

This was the moment that, according to popular vampire lore, a vampire was never supposed to see: sunrise. In fact, this notion was something a human had made up. What happens in the daylight is not destruction but a diminution of a vampire's powers. Vampires are strongest in the shadows, most powerful in the place that humans fear: the dark. They do not love the sun. In the light of day, the truth of their existence is impossible to deny. They are undead. In a world that lives and breathes and changes, they do not. Not truly a part of life and not life's true opposite, they are some strange combination of both.

They, I thought, and recognized my mistake. Old ways of thinking would no longer work.

We. Us. I made myself rephrase my thoughts.

It's happening, I realized. First my body, and now my brain and heart were accepting what had happened. *I am a vampire.*

I felt it then: the feeling that had propelled me from bed in the first place. A strange ache in all my limbs. An itchy sort of restlessness, as if my skin were suddenly stretched too tight across my bones. An urgency that gnawed. There was something I was supposed to do, some act I needed to perform. Once I had done it, everything would be all right. Abruptly, I realized that I was standing with my arms straight down at my sides, hands clenching and unclenching into tight fists. I folded my arms across my chest, and stuffed my hands into my armpits. In front of me, the sun catapulted over the horizon like a great burning ball.

Red. It was bloodred.

Oh, God, I thought, and felt the gnawing hunger become a painful twist of need inside my gut.

Blood. I needed blood. Not Ash's. Not the blood of another being like me. What my body needed, what it craved, was the one thing Ash couldn't give me. The taste that would make me undead forever: the taste of living blood.

Bloodlust. This is the beginning of the bloodlust, I thought.

I freed my arms to press them against my stomach, willing the pain, the desire, to recede. Was this the true reason vampires avoid the dawn? Because sunrise was really just the payoff of some enormous cosmic joke? The need for living blood strongest even as we begin to be diminished, our powers fading even as the sunlight brightens the world?

"Come back to bed, Candace," I heard Ash say. And as if just the sound of his voice had the ability to push my demons back, I felt the horrible, grinding need inside me ease, then slip away. I turned, walked to the bed, slipped between the sheets and into Ash's arms.

But first, I pulled the curtains closed to shut out the day.

Several hours later I loitered in the entryway of the Beijing's casino, idly watching the tourists as I waited for Ash. As we came downstairs in the elevator his cell phone had gone off; the call, one he indicated he had to take. I stopped at the concierge's desk to request Ash's car be brought up from the garage. The boxes containing our purchases of the day before now waited out by the curb. Under my previous circumstances, I would have joined them, enjoying the cool of the morning.

But not today. Today, I . . .

"Candace?" a voice behind me inquired.

I turned slowly, already knowing who I would find. I recognized the voice.

"Hello, Carl."

I hadn't seen Detective Carl Hagen in months, not since our awkward, painful breakup in a room at the morgue. Carl and I had dated pretty seriously for several months after I moved to Vegas. He was the first guy I had let touch me, the first one I'd wanted to touch me; the first I'd wanted to touch after San Francisco and that last near-fatal encounter with Ash. Having Carl suddenly turn up now seemed to bring things to some sort of strange full circle.

"It's good to see you," I said, and discovered as I said it that it was true. I took a moment to study him. Carl Hagen has always been one of the most driven, dedicated people I know. Now he looked . . . relaxed. His expression, less distracted. Fewer shadows darkened his eyes.

"You're looking well, Carl."

"Yeah?" he shrugged, and I couldn't help but smile. His work was the only thing about which Carl ever really felt comfortable accepting a compliment. I watched his steady gaze take in my appearance. "Same goes."

We stood for a moment while the air between us

hummed with unspoken thoughts. Should we try to continue the conversation or shake hands and go our separate ways? Carl and I hadn't exactly parted on the best of terms last time around. He had pretty much told me he couldn't trust me. He accused me of holding back information vital to a case he was working. He was right on both counts. The information I failed to share had to do with the existence of vampires, a situation Carl was still in the dark about. If I had anything to say about it, that's the way things would stay.

"I took some time off," he suddenly went on. "Just now getting back to the grind."

"Don't tell me," I said. "Fly-fishing in Montana?"

He grinned but shook his head, his eyes both pleased and surprised, as if he hadn't expected I would remember his love of fly-fishing. "Good guess," he acknowledged. "But no. I went east, helped my brother in Vermont on his Christmas tree farm."

"I didn't know you had a brother," I said, surprised in my own turn.

"Probably didn't mention him," Carl said simply. "In recent years, we sort of, I don't know, drifted apart. But after . . ." His voice trailed off, and I realized he'd been about to refer to our parting. "I guess

I figured maybe I hadn't tried hard enough and I should give things another shot. The worst that could happen is the same thing as last time."

"And what was that?"

"He told me I was a self-righteous prick and to go to hell."

I gave a quick laugh, suddenly feeling better than I had all morning. There was something so straightforward about Carl. It had been part of my attraction to him in the first place. It wasn't that he didn't have depths. He did. They just weren't hidden ones.

"I'm glad things worked out better this time around," I said.

He nodded. "Yeah. So am I."

He paused for a moment, his eyes on mine. And, suddenly, I knew what he wanted to say next. *Oh, don't,* I thought. *Not here. Not now. I don't want to hurt you again, Carl.*

"So what brings you here first thing in the morning?" he asked, shifting the course of our conversation as if he had sensed my silent plea. "You haven't changed jobs, have you? I can't imagine Al Manelli ever letting you go."

"No, I haven't," I said. "As a matter of fact, I—"

"Sorry that took so long."

Smooth and clean as a sharp knife, Ash's voice

cut through mine. He stepped up beside me, and I felt his hand come up to curl around my elbow. I started at his touch, as though I'd brushed against a live wire.

"Am I interrupting something?"

I watched Carl blink, just once, before his cop face slammed down. His expression became absolutely neutral. His eyes, watchful and intent. Not a trace of what he was, or wasn't, feeling showed.

"Not really," I said, as easily as I could. "I just had the good luck to bump into an old friend, that's all." I shifted ever so slightly, dislodging my elbow from Ash's grip, so that the three of us formed a triangle with me as the point. "I can't remember if the two of you have ever met," I went on. "Ash, this is Carl Hagen—*Detective* Carl Hagen, I should say. Carl, this is Ash Donahue. We knew each other in San Francisco, before I moved to Vegas."

"It's a pleasure," Ash said, extending his hand. Carl took it. I watched them perform a mano-a-mano handshake.

The formalities over, Ash's silver eyes flicked to mine and held. "Are you ready to go home, Candace?" he asked, quietly.

He didn't say *our home,* but then he didn't have to. The meaning was there, clear as the chime of a bell. All of a sudden, I realized how tired I was. Tired, and the human day was just beginning. *This is what it will be like from now on,* I thought. The interplay between my former life as a human and my new existence as a vampire. Every single sentence, every syllable of every single word would have a double meaning that only I would know. Carl didn't trust me because I concealed things. I wondered what his reaction would be if he knew what I was hiding from him now. Simply standing beside him made me feel like a liar.

"Yes," I said. "I'm ready." I extended my own hand toward Carl and he took it without hesitation, the grip strong and gentle all at once. Carl, himself, in a nutshell. "It was lovely to see you, Carl."

"You, too, Candace," he said. He gave my fingers one last, tight, squeeze, then let go. "Take care, now. I'll see you around."

With a nod to Ash, he walked past us. The casino's automatic doors *whooshed* open, and Carl stepped outside. I waited, Ash still as a statue beside me, until Carl had passed out of sight. Then I stepped through the doors myself, out into the light of the sun.

Both Ash and I were silent as he skillfully piloted the Mercedes through the Vegas streets. It wasn't until we reached the outskirts of town, on our way to the gated community where Ash—and now I—lived, that he spoke.

"Your detective is impressive."

I gave a mental sigh. Apparently, some things held constant for males whether living or undead. "He is impressive," I agreed, careful to keep my voice neutral. "He's just not mine."

Ash negotiated a turn, punched the accelerator. I could almost feel it leap like an animal straining against its tether.

"You're trying to tell me you weren't lovers?" Ash asked.

"Would you believe me if I did?"

"No."

"Then it will hardly do me any good to lie. For the record, what I did with Carl, or anyone else for that matter, can hardly be considered cheating on you, Ash. You weren't exactly in my life at the time."

Except in my memories, and in my dreams, I thought.

A car shot past us, the sun glinting off its windshield. I winced and shied my head away, closing my eyes. I kept them closed as the silence inside the car began to stretch. *It's like playing chicken,* I thought, and wondered if I would be considered the one to blink first if I gave in and spoke when my eyes were already closed.

"Were there others?" he asked, his voice tight, and I fought against a sudden, desperate impulse to laugh. I hadn't been the first to blink after all.

"Absolutely," I said. "So many, I lost count. Why do you think I moved to Vegas in the first place?"

I opened my eyes, turned toward him.

"Yes, Carl was my lover," I said, in a clear, concise voice. "A very good lover, in fact. I enjoyed him, and he enjoyed me. When he broke things off, I was sorry. Is that what you want to know?"

"Did you love him?"

"No."

Ash turned his head. For a split second, his silver eyes met mine, and I saw that they were filled with turmoil. Some tortured need to have an urgent question answered, a question he was unwilling, or unable, to ask aloud. His reaction to Carl wasn't simply some perverse and futile Y-chromosome-related need to dominate the past. There was something else going on. Something much more important. The only problem was that I didn't have the faintest idea what it was.

I reached out and laid a hand on his arm.

"No," I said once more. *The truth, the whole*

truth, and nothing but the truth will do, I thought.
"I never loved Carl Hagen, Ash, though I probably
should have. He's a great guy. I didn't love him but
I wanted him and I liked him. He was what I
needed . . . at the time."

"You mean he was alive."

"Yes," I said. "That's exactly what I mean."

Ash turned his face away then, and I let my arm
drop back into my lap. The gates of Ravenswood,
the exclusive community Ash had chosen as his
home base, came into view.

"Maybe you should have tried harder to love
him," he said softly as we approached, almost as if
he was speaking to himself. "If you had, you might
still be alive. If you were alive again, maybe you
would go back to him, work things out."

"Maybe," I replied as I felt a sudden pain shoot
straight through my heart. "There's just one little
problem: I'm not alive. And I love you, Ash. I did
then. I do now."

I leaned my head back against the seat, trying
to ignore the way the pain spread out, moving
through my veins like fast-acting poison. *Don't say
any more, Candace,* I thought, but I couldn't stop
myself.

"What's the matter? Tired of me already? Decided I'm not worth the effort after all?"

"No," Ash said quickly, his head whipping around. *"Damn it,"* he said, as he took in the expression on my face. "I'm doing this all wrong."

"I have no idea what you're doing, but I'm inclined to agree."

We reached the gates; the security guard leaned down to gaze into the car, then waved us through.

Ash waited until we were well inside Ravenswood, its stately houses and carefully manicured lawns all looking remarkably the same, before he spoke.

"I've been acting like an idiot, haven't I?"

"The thought did occur."

His eyes still on the road, Ash took one hand from the wheel and reached to capture one of mine. He pressed it to his lips, and I felt the heat of the kiss spread out, like an antidote to the poison of our conversation.

"I didn't mean to be," he said. "I apologize."

He took a corner, and the house came into sight. *Finally,* I thought. I felt myself relax for the first time since leaving the Beijing. We were home. Here I could get Ash to tell me what was really bothering him. Together, we would make it right. I got out of the car. Without warning, the world tilted. A wave of nausea crashed over me. Spots danced before my eyes. If I hadn't had my hand on the roof of the car, I would have dropped where I stood.

"*Ash!*" I cried, and even I could hear the panic in my own voice.

"It's all right, Candace," Ash said swiftly. "Remember, I warned you this might happen. You just need to feed, that's all."

I heard his quick footsteps then felt the world give another swoop as he picked me up, cradling me in his arms. I let my head fall back to rest against his shoulder.

"But I fed," I protested. To my horror, I could feel a sob pressing, sharp as a sudden pain, against the inside of my chest. "Just last night."

"And you've expended a lot of energy, both before and after," Ash said, his tone calm and patient as he started toward the front door. "You're body is still adjusting, and you've never been outside in daylight before. This morning was your first time. You need to feed, to get out of the sun and conserve your strength."

I did give a sob then as the pain in my chest went abruptly needle-sharp. My body seemed to be moving of its own accord. My mouth seeking Ash's throat.

Seeking skin. Seeking blood.

I clenched my eyes shut tightly, as if not seeing

him would drive the need back, force it down. Instead, I felt it ratchet up another notch. *I'm worse than an animal,* I thought. Driven by needs, by instincts that my mind could comprehend but not control. Vaguely, I realized that we had passed into the house. And then my hands were moving, scrabbling at Ash's shirt, desperate to expose more skin.

"Ash," I panted. "Ash, I need . . ."

"Go ahead, Candace."

I twisted in his arms so that I faced him, wrapping my legs around his waist, nuzzling his neck in a parody of passion. I felt Ash stop walking and simply sink down to the floor. In some dim corner of my mind, I realized we had made it no farther than the kitchen. Ash was sitting with his back against the stove. I tested my teeth against the taut skin of his throat, felt the way his body held firm, then gave way as I bit down. The taste of blood, the *reality* of it, flooded my senses, filled my mouth.

More, my body screamed. *More. More. More.* In that moment, it seemed to me that I could never get enough.

Over and over, I pulled mouthfuls of Ash's blood into my mouth. I felt Ash's arms around me tremble, then begin to shake. I knew I was pushing his body to its limits.

Stop, I commanded myself. *Candace, you have got to stop.*

With a cry of anguish, I wrenched my mouth away. Flung myself to one side, out of Ash's arms. I crawled a few paces away, then lay exhausted, one cheek pressed against the cool tiles of the kitchen floor, and waited to return to my right mind. Assuming I still had one.

Do something. Say something, I thought. Anything to make the situation bearable, less desperate and horrific than it was.

"Now that's what I call one hell of a morning after," I finally managed, and heard Ash make a strangled sound.

I wanted to roll over, roll back toward him, but found I didn't quite have the strength. It was so cool, so restful to simply lie without moving on the kitchen floor. My terrible need sated, for the time being at least. Ash's blood swimming through my body, making it strong, making it whole.

"Was that a laugh? Please say yes," I said.

"Yes," Ash replied.

A moment later, I heard him move, sliding over to stretch out beside me, pulling me back against him so that our bodies fit together like spoons. Such a simple, tender, human thing to do. Also, the last straw. I began to weep, tears streaming down my cheeks, my body racked with great, silent sobs.

"Candace," Ash said softly. "There's no need. Don't."

But I could not stop. *I need you, Ash,* I thought. *I need you so much.* Not just to love, but to survive. My thoughts circled like a frantic carousel inside my head.

One night. We had been given just one night to explore the world and each other, to celebrate our newfound existence, newly experienced love. One night, but no more. A night that had ended in a morning filled with desperation and blood.

My honeymoon with the vampire was over.

Six

"I have to say this," I said.

"Be my guest," Ash said pleasantly.

"Wow."

He gave a quick laugh as, together, we walked up the front steps of the house where the private auction would be held. A pair of lions that would have made the New York Public Library proud eyed us from either side. Until that moment, I hadn't realized how quickly accustomed I had become to the anonymity of the gated community where Ash lived. The way the homes, though huge, all sort of blended together with few distinguishing features, as if the people who lived there had decided it was in bad taste to stand out. This house was a different animal entirely.

"It looks like something straight out of Dickens or Brontë," I said as Ash and I reached the front door. Another lion's head greeted us in the form of an enormous knocker. Ash inserted two fingers into the lion's mouth, lifted the ring, then dropped it back down. The crack of metal on metal sounded loud as a gunshot.

"Actually," he said. "You're not far off. I believe Luther had the whole building taken apart in England then shipped to Vegas—lock, stock, and barrel. Then he had it reassembled and restored. I think he considered it just another part of his collection."

"Luther?" I said.

"The man whose collection we're here to dismantle. Luther Covington."

Ash and I had spent the daylight hours quietly, both of us conserving our strength. Ash had recovered quickly from the morning's events. It had taken me much longer, and even then my body had recovered more quickly than my mind. I knew enough to be afraid now. Afraid my own needs would betray me, afraid they would betray Ash. As if he sensed my need for privacy, Ash waited until the end of the day to seek me out. Then, as the sun slipped below the horizon, he came to me. Gently, Ash had stroked my fears aside. With his fingers, with his tongue, he had brought me back to myself. Until the world once again seemed like a kaleidoscope of passion and possibilities, all of them inextricably bound to him and to the setting of the sun.

*   *   *

"Ah, Mr. Donahue. Good evening, sir," a voice said as the front door swung inward. An elderly man in a tuxedo materialized in the opening, the quintessential butler.

"Good evening, Hughes," Ash said. There was genuine pleasure in his voice, and in the butler's, too. The more time I spent with Ash, the more I began to see that although he was primarily a loner, he nevertheless possessed the ability to draw people to him.

"Hughes," Ash said, "this is Miss Candace Steele. Candace, this is Peter Hughes, Mr. Covington's butler."

"It's a pleasure to meet you, Mr. Hughes," I said. I offered my hand, and he took it briefly in a firm grip.

"Please do come in," he said. "The viewing has already started."

We made our way toward the murmur of voices at the far end of the entry hall. Beneath our feet, the floor was an elaborate parquet. Game animal heads gazed down at us from walls covered with William Morris wallpaper. I wondered if Luther had shot the animals himself.

"So you're a friend of the family?" I asked.

"I wouldn't go that far," Ash replied as he captured my hand. "I met Luther not long after I came to Vegas," he explained. "We shared several interests, and he was generous enough to let me view his collection a number of times. It's entirely unique."

We reached the end of the hallway, turned to the right. "Ah! Here we are."

The high-ceilinged room before us had probably been the house's ballroom in its previous life. Ash and I paused at its entrance, two sets of double doors, both thrown open wide. I felt Ash's energy rev up a notch. *He's taking stock,* I thought. I stood beside him, trying to see the ballroom through his eyes.

The overall lighting in the room was soft, the better to highlight Luther Covington's treasures. Ash had hinted that I would find it an eclectic mix. He was absolutely right. Chinese vases of celadon green sat on high pedestals. Polished black Anasazi pots stood right alongside. Rows of paintings in all shapes and sizes ringed the walls. There were tapestries, furniture, and low glass-topped and glass-fronted cases containing I couldn't quite see what.

And around through them, like figures in a play, were men and women dressed in elegant evening clothes. Though not as overwhelming as the sensations that had pressed all around me in the casino, the figures in the room packed their own punches. Unless I very much missed my guess, some very big-time competition was going to take place here before the night was done.

All of a sudden, I realized I was grinning. *Let the games begin,* I thought. I linked my arm through Ash's.

"Show me everything," I said.

He smiled and reached to tuck my fingers even more firmly through the crook of his arm. "What would you like to see first?"

"I haven't any idea," I answered honestly as we crossed the threshold. On the left side of the room, the opposite direction from the one in which we were headed, a podium and series of padded folding chairs had been set up.

"Why don't we go look at whatever it is you want to bid on? What is it, by the way? I forgot to ask before."

"Heart scarabs," Ash said. "One in particular." He made a motion with his chin, to indicate the direction in which he wanted to go. "I think they're over there."

I accepted a glass of champagne from a passing waiter. "Okay," I said, "lead on."

I took a sip, my arm still linked with Ash's as we maneuvered through the room.

"A scarab," I echoed, frowning in an effort to recall what little I knew. "That means it's shaped like a beetle, right?"

"Right." Ash nodded. "Heart scarabs were ancient Egyptian funerary offerings. Usually, they're found inside the actual mummy wrappings."

"Don't tell me," I said. "Located right above the heart."

Ash smiled. "Well done. I'll make an expert of you yet. . . . Here we are."

We stopped in front of a small glass case in the far right corner of the room. Its wood was polished to a gleaming black and intricately carved. Inside it, illuminated by the internal lights, were a series of objects, each shaped like a beetle's back, the smallest no bigger than my thumbnail, the largest as big as my palm, but all carved from some variety of green stone. I leaned over the case to study the scarabs more closely, then jerked back, startled. Dozens of pairs of tiny eyes seemed to stare straight back into mine.

"They have human faces," I exclaimed.

"Many of them do, yes," Ash nodded. "It's one of their hallmarks." He leaned over the case in his turn now and, after a moment, I joined him, looking at the scarabs for a second time. They were no less eerie, but I could begin to see their beauty, and their variations.

"Which is the one you want?" I asked.

Ash pointed. "That one."

I leaned close again to study it. There was nothing to make this scarab stand out from any of the others, in my eyes. Its color was dark, so dark I almost couldn't see the human face incised upon it. It was medium-size. If I could have held it, it would have nestled comfortably in the very center of my palm.

"Why that one?"

"Because it's the right one," Ash said. He said it in a casual tone without emphasis. But call it rapport or intuition, I sensed that this scarab was extremely important to Ash.

"The right one for what?" I also tried to sound casual.

He gave me a smile that didn't quite reach his eyes.

"Never ask a collector to explain why he wants something, Candace. Not only will you never get a straight answer, you'll get a different one every time."

"But you want this for yourself," I persisted. "Not for a client."

Ash hesitated for a fraction of a second before he nodded. I could almost hear a door between us slam shut.

"I often purchase objects that interest me personally, adding them to my own collection while I wait for the right buyer to come along. It's not so unusual. Many dealers do it."

"The ancient Egyptians believed that the heart was the most essential organ in the body," Ash went on. "Not because it pumped blood, but because it was considered the seat of rational thought. The heart was the origin of all actions, all feelings. Upon death of a mortal, the gods of the Underworld weighed it to determine whether or not a spirit was worthy to enter the afterlife, because it was in the heart that all memory of the person's deeds on earth were stored."

There's something he's not telling me, I thought. *Something important.* Ash had done this before. Always because he was trying to protect me from something. What was it this time?

"I have to go take care of some paperwork," Ash said. "Do you want to keep looking, or tag along?"

"I think I'll keep looking," I said, careful to keep my tone light. "I saw some jewelry back there. Maybe I'll go pick out something. A piece that feels like the 'right one.' Then we'll see just how much you really love me."

He dropped a quick kiss on my lips. "You do that," he said. I watched him as he sauntered off. Then I turned back to the case with the scarabs, studying the one Ash intended to bid on. *Why this one, Ash?* I wondered once more. *What is its secret?* What don't you want me to know?

Until a few moments ago, I had assumed that

Ash's attendance at the auction tonight was strictly business. Now I couldn't help but wonder if it wasn't something more. Of course, his unwillingness to explain why he wanted the scarab *could* stem from the fact that we were out in public, nothing more. Ash played everything close to the vest. His reluctance to explain might arise from nothing more complicated than a desire to not be overheard. Maybe I was just letting my imagination get the better of me.

And maybe not.

I turned, determined to spend some time looking at things that sparkled instead of creepy human-faced bugs, took two steps, and ran smack into the person who had come up behind me without my realizing it. So much for my vampire powers.

"I'm so sorry," I exclaimed.

"Well, at least I know it's really you," said the person I nearly stepped on.

I felt my stomach give a sudden lurch of joy, followed by one of dismay, then one of guilt.

"What are you doing here?" I blurted out.

"Well, it's nice to see you, too," my friend Bibi Schwartz answered with a laugh. "Thank you very much. I was going to tell you how great you looked. Just for that, I think I'll just be keeping that information to myself."

"I'll say it instead," I said. "You look great."

"Say the rest," Bibi prompted, her dark eyes grinning.

"But then you always do."

"Now that's the Candace Steele I know and love."

Bibi was wearing a column of shimmering white, which perfectly set off her dark coloring. She closed the gap between us to give me a hug. I hugged back and felt the guilt rise up to clog my throat.

"I should be asking what *you're* doing here," she said, linking her arm through mine. "Not to mention giving you hell for not returning my calls. But I'm too happy to see you. Actually, I'm just too happy in general. Come over here and look at some of this jewelry. Is this whole thing outrageous, or what?"

I didn't resist. I was hoping she would keep talking and give me time to collect my badly scattered thoughts. I've known Bibi since my San Francisco days when she lived right down the hall from me. She was the one who put me back together after Ash attacked me in the elevator. She's not exactly his biggest fan. In a gathering this size, the chance that Bibi and Ash would fail to spot each other was next to none. The miracle was that she hadn't spotted him already.

"That dress really is fabulous, by the way," she went on as we made our way across the room. Wired energy poured off her in waves. She kept turning her head from side to side, as if searching the room for someone. Abruptly, I felt my nerves steady as I realized why.

She's here with Randolph, I thought.

Randolph Glass is the owner of the Scheherazade, the casino where I work. Bibi and Randolph are a couple despite the fact that Randolph is married to a rich woman he will never divorce. When Bibi recently broke things off with him, I was the first to applaud and offer support. Since then, Randolph had been away, raising money for a new casino. But now, unless I very much missed my guess, Randolph was back, and Bibi was back in his arms.

"Where the hell have you been, anyway?" she asked. "I thought you were going to come and see my show."

"I am," I said as we reached the jewelry cases. "But you know I had a few days off."

"Well, sure," Bibi said. "But I didn't think you'd completely drop out of sight." All of a sudden, her eyes widened as she swung back around to face me. I could practically hear the coin drop.

"You're seeing someone new, aren't you?" she

whispered as her grip on my arm tightened in excitement. "That's why you've been flying below the radar. And he's brought you here tonight. Where is he? *Who* is he? Details. I want every single one."

Oh, no you don't, I thought.

"I should have known I'd find you looking at jewelry," a voice behind me said, one I recognized.

"Good evening, Candace," Randolph said as I swung around to face him.

"Good evening," I responded. "Welcome home," I went on. "I hope your trip went well."

I heard Bibi suck in a breath. Randolph simply smiled. He cocked his head in Bibi's direction, as if asking a question, and she released my arm, though she stayed right where she was. I felt a swift stab of fury, understanding the unspoken signal at once. *You bastard,* I thought. He was playing one of the oldest power games in the book, and my least favorite: taking sides.

"Very well, thank you," Randolph Glass replied. I watched as his gaze swept over me in a deliberate assessment, or maybe that should be reassessment. "What brings you here tonight?"

Translation: *You're a little out of your league, aren't you? Even if you are all dressed up.* I might actually have enjoyed the sparring, if Bibi hadn't been involved. At this point, she could only get hurt. I was about to stick a knife in her all by myself.

"A close friend is an antiquities dealer," I answered calmly, my eyes steady on Randolph's, even as I heard Bibi catch her breath once more. And now she did shift position, taking a step away from me, toward Randolph. It was what I'd expected, but it hurt anyhow. Undead didn't equal unfeeling. "I'm here as his guest."

Randolph's eyes narrowed just a fraction. I could almost hear the wheels turn inside his mind. He reached out, slid his fingers down one of Bibi's arms till his hand met hers, then tugged her to his side.

"How interesting," he remarked. "I wonder if I know him."

"I have no idea," I replied. "He hasn't been in Vegas long." Ash had been present at Randolph's New Year's gathering, but his purpose had hardly been to socialize with the host. I knew a certain amount of meet and greet went on at such functions, but I didn't know if the two had done any more than exchange a brief hello.

I saw a spasm of emotion cross Bibi's face, and knew what was coming, even if my own senses hadn't already informed me of Ash's approach.

"There you are," I heard his voice say, right on

cue. I sensed rather than heard him come up behind me to lay the fingers of one hand lightly on my
shoulder. "You found someone you know. How
nice. Hello, Bibi. Always a pleasure to run into
you."

Bibi's face had gone as white as her dress. She
clearly looked wounded, fearful, and incredibly
pissed off. A hard combination to manage, but
then Bibi does have talent.

"Ash," she responded.

"I'm not sure you know Randolph Glass," I
said, picking up the introductions ball. "Randolph,
this is the friend I was telling you about."

"Ash Donahue," Ash said as he stepped to my
side. He extended his hand. I had a strange sense of
déjà vu as I watched Randolph's hand swing up to
meet it. This was essentially the same ritual Ash
and Carl had performed, though with somewhat
different overtones.

"Actually, I believe we have met before," Ash
went on. "I had the pleasure of being at your home
on New Year's Eve."

"I'm glad you enjoyed yourself," Randolph
replied. *Okay, points for you,* I thought. "Candace
tells me you're an antiquities dealer," he went on.

"Donahue and Associates," Ash answered, then
he grinned. "I'd be happy to give you my card."

Randolph gave a quick laugh, as if Ash's own response had measured up. "I'll consider it," he said. "The casino hosts a variety of exhibitions, as you must know. But I'm thinking of starting a more personal collection. It's one of the reasons we're here tonight."

"Any particular area of focus?" Ash inquired.

Randolph shrugged but his eyes stayed sharp. "I'm trying to stay open about that," he said.

"You've come to the right place, then," Ash said easily. "With that approach, you'll be a collector after Luther Covington's heart."

"Ladies and gentlemen, if you'll excuse me—" a smooth voice said. As a group, we turned to find one of the tuxedo-clad waiters standing nearby. "We've just been informed that we're ready to begin. If I could encourage you to select places near the podium . . ."

"Thanks. We'll do that," Ash said. He took my arm. "A pleasure to see you both again," he said to Bibi and Randolph. "If you decide you'd like to use my services, Candace will know where to find me."

"Good luck," Randolph said.

"And to you," Ash replied.

Bibi and Randolph moved away first. Ash and I held our ground. If we had all proceeded together, we might have felt compelled to sit together, too.

Now that would have been a lot of fun. Bibi looked back, just once, casting a long look over her shoulder. Her eyes resting first on Ash, then moving on to me. They spoke volumes.

"What a fortunate thing it is that looks can't actually kill," Ash remarked. "If they could, Bibi would have me buried six feet under."

"I'd appreciate it if you wouldn't joke about this situation," I said as we walked toward the podium. "What Bibi thinks may not be important to you, but it is to me. Losing my friendship with Bibi is going to be difficult enough without you poking fun."

"I apologize," Ash said at once. He was silent for a moment, as we selected our seats, second row from the back, on the left-hand aisle. I could see Bibi and Randolph closer to the front and on the right. Bibi's back was straight as a fireplace poker. "Believe it or not, I actually thought joking might help."

"No," I said simply. "It doesn't."

"Then I stand corrected and it won't happen again."

"You make it awfully difficult to stay angry with you," I remarked after a moment.

Ash turned his head to look at me directly. "Is being angry with me what you want?"

"No," I said again. "No, it isn't. It's just . . . The

situation with Bibi is complicated. Deciding how I feel may take some time. Now let's stop talking about it, so I can enjoy what we came for."

I saw the smile come back into Ash's eyes. "And what is that?" he inquired.

"Simple," I said. "Watching rich people fight to the death while pretending they're doing something much more civilized."

With Ash's arm around my shoulders, I settled back in my seat to concentrate on the auction.

Half an hour later, I was back to enjoying myself. The fears, the pain of seeing Bibi, not forgotten but allowed to rest quietly in the back of my mind. It hardly takes a Ph.D. to figure out that Vegas is a town that runs on money. But I had been telling Ash the truth when I said I was looking forward to watching the wealthy at play. Even if the color of the blood in your veins is blue, the color of money still talks.

The auctioneer finished with Luther Covington's collection of Anasazi pots, took a calm sip of water, and consulted his notes.

"Ladies and gentlemen, we move now to ancient Egypt and a collection of heart scarabs. The first item in this group is listed in your catalog as number four seven five."

There was a rustle of paper as the attendees consulted the catalog notes while one of the auction-eer's elegantly attired assistants held the scarab up for view. Even from a distance, I could see this was not the item Ash intended to bid on. This one was large, a pale green. So far, Ash was biding his time, seeming more than content to wait and watch others do polite battle for what they desired. I wondered if he would have much competition when his time came. I had something of an answer when, to my surprise, bidding for the first scarab was brisk and spirited. Eventually, it went to a small, dapper man sitting not far from Bibi and Randolph.

"Do you know him?" I murmured quietly.

"Not personally," Ash replied. "But I certainly know him by reputation. Most of his clients are museums."

As we spoke, a ripple of motion in the right-hand section of seats caught my eye. A latecomer, his dark hair—long enough to brush the top of his tuxedo jacket collar—was moving quietly yet with purpose up the far right aisle. Though he was careful not to disturb the other guests, obviously not seeking attention, I couldn't take my eyes off him. Everything about him seemed clear and precise, as if the shape of him had been cut out of the air by a thin, sharp knife.

Vampire, I thought.

Ash cocked his head in the newcomer's direction,

as if the other vampire's presence made an actual sound. I felt his body go alert, a current of something I couldn't quite put a name to humming through it. But he didn't turn to look. Instead, he kept his gaze focused on the podium. If the newcomer realized he wasn't the only vampire present, he gave no sign. As I watched, he slid into a vacant seat about halfway to the podium, on the far aisle. Just before he sank down into it, he shifted, turning his body so that he could gaze out over the back half of the assembled guests. I felt a stab of horror shoot straight down my spine.

Along the right side of his face, hidden from my view until that moment, ran a long, jagged scar. My hands went clammy and my head felt light.

"Ash," I managed to get out.

Ash turned his head then and looked at the vampire. I knew the second their eyes met. An arc of pure energy seemed to sizzle through the air, so intense I all but saw the spark. Then the second vampire smiled, a flash of perfect, even teeth, before sinking down into the chair, back to us, face to the podium.

"That's him. That's the one who attacked me," I whispered, even though I wanted to shout.

I felt Ash's energy leap, like a mastiff straining against a leash. "You're sure?" he asked at once, careful to keep his own voice low.

"Positive," I replied. "There can't be *that* many vamps sporting that particular combination. Dark hair, facial scar. Remember, I told you I marked him myself, four nights ago. It's how I got him to back off."

Ash made a hissing sound through his teeth, and I pulled my eyes away from the other vampire to the one at my side. Ash's always pale face had gone dead white with fury.

"You know him, don't you?" I suddenly said.

Ash shot me a quick glance, and I saw the molten silver of his eyes. "We've met," he responded, his own voice expressionless. "In San Francisco. His name is Sloane."

Sloane, I thought. Without warning, my neck began to throb, as if remembering the grip of his teeth. My arms began to tremble, as if the sight of the scar Sloane now carried brought with it a sense memory of how it had come about. I could almost feel the sudden, miraculous drag of the silver as it had made its way down his face. The stench of flesh seemed to rise in my nostrils.

Bidding on the next heart scarab commenced. I barely noticed.

"Candace," Ash said after a moment. He reached to place one of his hands over mine, and it was only then that I realized how tightly I was gripping them together in my lap. I forced them to relax, then turned the top one palm up to lace my fingers with Ash's.

"I want to ask you to do something for me," he said. "It won't be easy. I'm going to ask it anyhow."

"What?"

"I want you to let me handle this situation. At least for now. It may be better for us if he thinks you don't recognize him. But you may have to meet him, do the small-talk thing before the night is out. Can you do that?"

"Just tell me one thing," I said. "Sooner or later, are we going to take him out?"

Ash smiled. "Oh, yes," he said. "Sloane will be made to pay for what he's done. You can count on it."

"Then I can do whatever it takes," I said.

He gave my hand a quick squeeze then released it. In the next moment, I understood why. At the front of the room, a third heart scarab was being held up for display prior to its auction. I recognized it at once. Dark and small, this was the scarab that Ash intended to bid on. I wondered who his competition would be. Other than Sloane, of course. There was no way the timing of his arrival was simple coincidence.

"Item four seven seven, ladies and gentlemen," the auctioneer was saying now. "One of the most unusual of the heart scarabs in the collection, due to its color and the detail of its ornamentation."

Bidding commenced. For one breathless moment, not a soul in the room moved, as if neither Sloane nor Ash wanted to be the first to tip his hand. Then the museum collector whose successful bid had won him the first scarab raised his paddle to display his number. Instantly, Ash raised his own, number 8. Sloane, number 25, topped Ash's bid. For several minutes the three men engaged in the most spirited bidding the evening had yet seen. Then, presumably having reached his spending limit, the museum collector abruptly shook his head. Now, it was just Sloane and Ash. I heard a murmur move through the room as the bids climbed into the triple digits.

"Four hundred thousand dollars, the bid stands at four hundred thousand to bidder number eight," the auctioneer said. An expectant hush fell across the assembled guests. Again, the auctioneer called out the amount, inviting any additional bids. He lifted the wooden gavel, the traditional tool for signaling the end of a bidding session. I risked a glance at Sloane to catch his reaction at Ash's victory.

"Five hundred thousand," a voice suddenly spoke out.

A startled murmur filled the room then quickly hushed. Again, the auctioneer called out the bid, inviting other participants to go higher. Ash's body hummed with tension but he stayed absolutely still.

"Sold," the auctioneer finally announced, bringing the gavel down with a *crack*. "To bidder number thirteen."

Lucky number thirteen, I thought.

Randolph Glass's number.

Seven

"Congratulations," Ash said agreeably some time later as he and Randolph Glass shook hands. The auctioneer was taking a break. The guests were on their feet, discreetly stretching, sauntering around the room. Waiters once again threaded through the crowd, offering food and drink. It seemed that spending money, or even just watching others do it, was hungry work. I saw more than a few glances aimed in our direction. Watching to see how the loser took it was always good sport.

"It's a fascinating piece," Ash was saying. "An excellent way to begin that private collection we were discussing earlier."

"I'm glad you think so," Randolph said. His eyes were gleaming with undisguised triumph.

He doesn't give a damn about that scarab, I realized suddenly. What Randolph cared about was beating Ash. *How can Bibi think for a moment she loves this guy?* I wondered. But then, no doubt, she wondered the same thing about me. At the moment

she was on the other side of the room. I didn't
know if it was her idea or Randolph's.

"If you decide not to make it a permanent acqui-
sition . . ." Ash began.

"You'll be the first to know," Randolph said
smoothly. "There's a very good chance we may be
able to come to terms. But I'd prefer to save that
discussion for a future occasion, if you don't mind.
Perhaps you and Candace could join us for dinner
some evening, after one of Bibi's shows."

"I'm sure we would both enjoy that," Ash said.

"Then, if you'll excuse me . . ." Randolph let his
voice trail off. *Important man. Places to go. People
to see. And I did just beat you, after all.*

"Of course," Ash said.

"Slimy bastard," I muttered under my breath, as
he moved off.

"But so predictably human," Ash said. "Now
that he's flexed his muscles, my guess is he'll part
with the scarab without too much fuss. Probably
the purpose of that dinner invitation, in fact. We'll
give it a day or so then follow up. I hope you won't
mind having dinner with the boss."

"Not at all," I said. "Maybe I'll get lucky and get
the chance to stab him with my steak knife. Rare
steak, of course."

Ash smiled and ran a hand down my arm. The
second he touched me, I knew what was coming

next. Together, as if we had choreographed it ahead of time, we turned to face Ash's other competitor.

"Hello, Sloane," Ash said. His voice sounded warm, almost pleased. Just for a moment, he let his eyes linger on the other vampire's face, on the scar I'd put there myself. "You've looked better."

Sloane grinned like a shark. "Hello, Ash. You're looking well. Too bad it won't last long. I've been asked to see to that, personally, by the way."

"You always were good at doing what you're told."

Sloane's eyes narrowed, and I could tell that Ash's barb had hit home. I might not have understood the context of their conversation, but one thing was as clear as glass: These two hated each other.

Without warning, almost as if he was changing tactics, Sloane's gaze shifted to me, his expression flat and predatory. *He has a shark's eyes, too,* I thought. But I could see, suddenly, that Sloane was a follower, not a leader.

"This must be the lovely Ms. Steele," Sloane said at last. "I'm so pleased to officially meet you at last."

You clever son of a bitch, I thought. The fact that we'd never been officially introduced didn't mean we hadn't met before. My belief that the attack on me had been random was growing slimmer with every second I spent in Sloane's company.

"Likewise," I said aloud.

"A pity about the scarab," Sloane went on, his gaze on Ash once more. "Particularly since that wealthy idiot has no idea what it is he's just acquired. How does it feel to lose, Ash?"

"Do you plan to stay in Vegas long, Mr. Sloane?" I asked before Ash could respond.

I felt a subtle current of energy move through Ash then. Whether it was approval or disapproval, I couldn't quite tell.

"Sloane," the other vampire said. "Just Sloane. And to answer your question, Ms. Steele, I'll be in Vegas for as long as it takes."

"You mean, to get the job done," Ash said.

Something flashed in Sloane's eyes, and suddenly I remembered what it had been like to lie in the rain-drenched street with my life's blood running down his throat. There'd been no finesse in that attack, just sheer brute force. *He enjoys what he is,* I thought. *The power and the pain of it.*

"That is what I mean, of course. And now, if you'll excuse me, I think I'll see what other entertainment I can find. What's that delightful cliché? Oh, yes, the night is young."

And unless I missed my guess, there would be another body in the city morgue before the night was done. With a final smile, Sloane moved off. I watched him pluck a glass of champagne from a nearby server and murmur something to her that made her blush. All of a sudden, I'd had more than enough.

"Do we have to stay?" I asked Ash.

"No, we don't," Ash said. "Let me take you home."

"Ash," I said quietly as he piloted the car through the neon Vegas night. "What aren't you telling me?"

I had waited until we were more than halfway home before I spoke; until the car was so filled with a thick, brooding tension I couldn't stand it any longer. The most disturbing thing about it was my sense that Ash, always so guarded, always so careful, had no idea he was even sending it out. On the bright side, he now trusted me so completely he knew he didn't need to shield his feelings from me. On the less than bright side, whatever was wrong, whatever was coming, was so bad that Ash couldn't completely control his dread.

"I can't tell you," he finally responded.

In spite of myself, I bit back a laugh. "You think this is funny?"

"Of course I don't think it's funny," I said. "But

you're not exactly giving me much room to maneuver. I can't help if you won't let me in."

"It's complicated," he said. "I seem to remember you saying that."

"About a situation you know virtually everything about already," I came back. "Look, I know we hardly have a no-secrets arrangement, but I've already had one less-than-delightful encounter with your friend Sloane. If he's a threat to me, or to you, don't you think I have the right to know? How the hell else am I supposed to protect myself, Ash?"

"He's not my friend," Ash said quickly. "And I don't want you to have to protect yourself. That's part of the problem."

"Nice wish, but I'd say it's just a little late." I turned my head to study his profile in the ambient glow of the lights.

"Ash, how did he know my name?"

Ash kept his eyes on the road ahead of us, the scattered lights of homes breaking the vast darkness of the desert.

"Okay," I said, unwilling to let him get away with silence. "There are a few possibilities. Someone at the auction told him my name."

"No," Ash said, his voice flat.

I felt fear grip my gut then at the only conclusion: Sloane had known about me for some time. "Then his attack on me wasn't random?"

"No," Ash said again.

"And," I hazarded a guess, "the reason I was his target has something to do with you."

"Yes."

I thought back to their cryptic conversation. "So what is it that he's been asked to see to personally? What did you mean when you said he was good at doing what's he told?"

"Just that," Ash replied.

"No, not just that. Who's giving him his orders? And what the hell is this all about?"

Ash stopped for a red light and turned to face me, his eyes hard and cold. "Sloane is here on behalf of others—other vampires. That is what makes him so dangerous. That is why I can't tell you anything more. So please, Candace, change the damn subject." The light turned green, and he started driving again.

"Should we talk about the weather?" I asked in sugary tones.

Without warning, Ash lifted one hand, brought it down, hard, open-palmed against the steering wheel. "Oh, fuck me," he said. He took the same hand, ran it through his hair in a gesture of sheer unadulterated frustration.

"Okay, but you're going to have to pull over," I said.

His head whipped in my direction, silver eyes

shining. For several seconds, nothing happened. Then I heard him give a strangled laugh.

I couldn't let it go. "One more question. Is this about the Board?"

I waited for Ash to explode as he did the last time I asked him about the Board. I was fishing then and fishing now. I know nothing about the Board. I had only surmised that the Board was a secret organization of powerful vampires.

He didn't explode. His voice was quiet, sad.

"Do you trust me?" he asked.

"Oh, for crying out loud," I began. "Please don't tell me you're going to do *that*."

"Do you?"

"How many times do I have to say it? Yes."

"Then give me more time," Ash said. "I'm not keeping you in the dark because I don't trust you. I'm trying— I want—" He gave his head a shake, as if to shake loose the words he wanted.

"It's dirty, Candace," he finally said. "It's ugly and vicious and I want to keep you out of it if I can. I don't want us to start whatever we can have together with this hanging over our heads. But until I can figure out a way to stop it, it's better if I don't explain."

"I don't like being kept in the dark," I said.

"I know," Ash said quickly. "I know that. In

your position, I'd no doubt feel the same. I wouldn't ask it of you now without a good reason. But I am. Please, Candace, if you love me, let me handle this in my own way."

"Low blow. You know damn well there's no *if* about it," I said. "How come guys always have to fight dirty in order to win?"

"Experience," Ash said. He slowed the car to take a corner. "For the record, we can do other things."

I leaned back against the headrest. There was really no question about what my answer would be. I would give Ash what he asked. Not because he had boxed me in, but because I thought I knew how much he hadn't wanted to. I turned toward him, slid a hand across his leg toward the notch of his thighs.

"Why don't you tell me all about that?"

I awoke, rearing up in bed like a swimmer breaking the surface of choppy water, desperate to escape drowning. My ears rang with a strange and sudden rush of sound. My tongue was thick and hot, the taste in my mouth salty, coppery. As always in the nighttime hours, the room I shared with Ash was pitch-black, but red spots danced in the air before my eyes. Bright red. Bloodred.

Blood, I thought. That's what the taste was. The sound of rushing in my ears. Blood. All blood. And as if the naming of it had released its hidden power, it seemed to me that I could feel it coursing through my veins. Nourishing me, making my vampire senses sharper. Without warning, my body spasmed once again, every sensation unbearably heightened. My hands clutched the sheets, just as they did in passion, my body bowed upward. Balanced on the edge of a knife, the split second before fulfillment overtakes desire. And then my vision went a high and blinding white as my whole body rode a wave of surging power. I was more than strong. I was invincible. No force on earth could stop me.

"Ash," I gasped out, though I knew now that he was not beside me. He was out, in what remained of the night. Protecting me, protecting us, with the most elemental means at his disposal. By continuing his own existence. By taking living blood.

I felt my body relax then, as the first wave of feeling passed, though my senses continued to hum. I reached out my hand, placed it in the center of the pillow where Ash's head usually lay.

Oh, Ash, I thought.

He was somewhere in the night, doing what needed to be done. And I would do no less. I closed my eyes and waited for the rising of the sun.

"Thanks for making time to see me, Al," I said as I slid into the booth at the coffee shop the next morning. Across the table from me, my boss at the Scheherazade gave a grunt. Al Manelli is not what one would call a morning person. It's one of the things we've always had in common.

"I ordered you some coffee," he said by way of greeting.

"Thanks," I said. Al took a sip of his own, eyes gazing at me over the rim of his mug. He might look and sound like he wanted to be home in bed. Most likely, he did. But his eyes were clear and sharp.

"So, Nerves," he said, using his favorite nickname for me as he set the mug down. Nerves for Nerves of Steel. The *e* on the end is optional. "What's up that couldn't wait until tonight?"

Tonight was the night I was supposed to report back to work at the Sher, but under the present circumstances, my returning to my regular evening rotation was not going to be in anyone's best interests. The question was, how to break this news to Al without going into detail about what was going on.

"That's what I want to talk about," I said. Al gave a second grunt. I took a sip of coffee, to buy myself an instant's more time. Seeing Al in person was proving more difficult than I had thought.

What would Al do, how would he feel, if he knew I had become a vampire?

"Al," I finally said, "I can't come back tonight. I've had some things come up—personal things. I need to handle them before I go back into the rotation. I know this is short notice, and I'm sorry."

There, I'd done it. Al was silent, studying me from across the table. Finally he spoke. "How much more time?"

"I don't know. I'm sorry."

"Stop apologizing," he said at once, his own voice testy. He took a sip of coffee, as if it would help him swallow down his temper. "What's this about, Candace? You in some kind of trouble?"

"Not really," I said. "No."

He gave a bark of unamused laughter. "That's not saying very much."

"There isn't a whole lot to say," I answered honestly. All of a sudden, I reached across the table to capture one of Al's hands. They were warm. Not just from the coffee cup, but because he was a living, breathing human being.

"Please, Al," I said. "I can't explain, but I really need you to trust me. Just give me some more time and I'll never ask for anything else, I swear to God."

"Okay, that's it," Al Manelli announced, even as his fingers curled around mine. "Now I know you're in trouble." He moved his other hand to cover mine. "What the hell is the matter with you, Steele? Your hands are as cold as ice."

"Yes or no, Al?"

He blew out an exasperated breath and released my hand. "Yes," he said. "And you damn well know it. But that doesn't mean I have to like it. How the hell can I watch your back if I don't know where you are?"

"I don't need you to watch my back," I said. "Whatever I have to do, it has to be alone. I really appreciate this, Al."

Al took another sip of coffee. "What do you want me to tell Randolph? He may not be the president of your fan club, but if you drop out of sight, he's bound to notice. And Bibi's going to want to know what's going on."

"Bibi is personal. You can leave her to me," I said. "As for Randolph, tell him I asked for some personal leave. I don't think he'll be surprised."

Al's eyebrows practically sailed right off his face, they rose so high. "This has something to do with Randolph?"

"It has to do with me, Al. But I ran into Randolph at some fancy auction last night. He thinks I'm screwing some high roller. If I suddenly ask for some time away, he may not be all that surprised."

"And are you?"

"None of your beeswax," I said, and won a reluctant smile. All of a sudden, I realized I was swallowing a lump in my throat. Al was one of the most important people in my new life in Vegas. I would miss seeing him, not just because he was my boss, but because he was my friend, my ally.

"You'll let me know when you're ready to come back?" he asked.

"I will," I promised.

"Then I'll square it away on the casino's end," Al replied. "And if there's anything else I can do, you let me know."

"I will," I said again, though I knew it was a lie. "This is more than enough. Thank you, Al." I began to slide from the booth. "I'd better go now. Anyone asks, tell them I snagged a rich millionaire and he's requested I stay off my feet for a while."

Al gave a snort. "I might just do that," he said. "You stay safe now, Nerves."

"That's the plan. Thanks again, Al. I won't forget this."

I stood then walked out of the coffee shop without looking back.

The meeting with Al over, I had one more important errand. I drove to my house. My house was more than simply where I ate, slept, did the laundry. It was the nerve center in my crusade against vampires.

I opened the door to the house then paused to let the world steady as it circled and spun. *Take it easy, Candace,* I thought. *Don't push yourself. Remember what happened last time.* Aside from the obvious need to conserve my energy during daylight hours, there was no need for me to rush. I checked my watch, figuring I had about ten minutes before the person I had asked to meet me here showed up. Time enough to do what needed to be done.

I moved through my house, making my way toward the secret room I had constructed with my own hands. The room that contained every single thing I knew about vampires and how to fight them. I triggered the mechanism to release the door, stepped inside what I always thought of as my office. Like the rest of the house, the air of this room was still and close. Out of habit more than anything else, I secured the door behind me, then stood for a moment, taking stock.

In front of me was my desk with its high-end laptop. Bookshelves filled with research materials. Drawers for weapons of varying shapes and kinds. And, directly across from the desk, the focal point of the room, my cork situation board, empty except for a single item: the sketch of Ash that he had given me in San Francisco, the one with the strange insignia and characters on the back that I had never been able to decipher. I had left it there following the events that had culminated in the death of Senator Cabot Hamlyn on New Year's Eve at Randolph Glass's house, a reminder of unfinished business.

I set the shoulder bag I carried with me down on the desk then walked across the room to the cork-board. I unpinned Ash's image, stood looking at his face. *Everything always comes back to you, Ash, doesn't it?* I thought.

And, in that moment, I felt the world tilt as I suddenly saw my life in a way I never had before. Even this room, which I had built so painstakingly, so certain I was creating something for myself alone, even this had Ash as its center. *Why had I never realized how thoroughly his presence permeated every part of my existence?* It was true that I had come to Vegas because of my friendship with Bibi, but my real reason for leaving San Francisco had been to start over, to begin a new life after what had happened between me and Ash. The awakening of our love. Its ultimate, almost fatal consequences. I thought I had succeeded, in this room most of all.

Now, in a flash of intuition so precipitous it left me dizzy, I realized the truth. I hadn't started over. Not for one moment. Not at all. From the moment we met, Ash had become the pivot point of my existence. All the decisions I made in Vegas—the creation of my hidden office, my personal crusade to eliminate vampires who fed on human blood—were bound to him. He was their cause, their reference point.

Without Ash, I would have had no reason to fear vampires, no desire to destroy them. If not for Ash, I would have been just like everybody else. But because of him, I was different forever. Forever marked and set apart. Now and always, the same amount of time he had sworn to love me, there would be no existence without him. The only way to be free of Ash would be to die.

Well, this is useful, Candace, I thought. *Just what, precisely, are you so upset about? You had your shot at ending it. You didn't take it. You didn't want to die.*

Instead, I begged Ash not to let me go.

I felt my gut clench then as a pang of need shot through it. A need for Ash. A need for blood. My fingers gripped the drawing of Ash, wrinkling the edges of the dry, old paper before shoving it into my shoulder bag.

I can't give in to this, I thought. I had to fight the blood craving, even if it meant fighting both Ash and myself. I was tired of feeling weak, of being weak. I wanted what I thought I had created in Vegas: a life I chose and controlled.

From the front of the house, I heard the muffled sound of the doorbell chime. I went to answer the door.

"Thanks for coming, Chet," I said a few moments later as the Sher's computer security guru and I stood in the living room. "I really appreciate it."

"Not a problem," said Chet McGuire. He swallowed, and I watched the way his Adam's apple bobbed up and down in his skinny throat. Chet looks like the quintessential socially inept computer geek, but I knew there was a whole lot more to him.

"So." He ran his palms down the front of his pants, as if suddenly realizing they were sweaty. "You said you needed my help?"

"I do, yes," I replied. "But there are a couple of conditions."

"Parameters," Chet said at once. "Let's call them that. I'm good with parameters."

"Parameters it is, then," I said.

Chet smiled and his Adam's apple stilled. "Okay," he said. "Bring 'em on."

Though he had worked at the Sher longer than I had, the first time I met Chet was over the winter, when he helped foil a particularly nasty vampire plot involving an attack on a United States senator.

He saved my life, in fact. In the process, I had learned that Chet also has a personal grudge against vampires. They had taken his best friend before his very eyes. His hatred of them ran just as deep as mine; he was the perfect person for the favor I was about to ask.

"The parameters are really pretty basic," I said. "I need you to keep absolutely everything about today's visit, including the fact that I asked you to come here at all, to yourself. In particular, you are not to tell Bibi."

Behind his Coke-bottle glasses, Chet's eyes grew wide. Since the events of the winter, he and Bibi and I had formed a loose triumvirate of sorts. He knew that Bibi and I were close, knew how unusual it would be for me to keep anything from her. As quickly as they had grown wide, his eyes narrowed in comprehension.

"This has to do with vampires, doesn't it?"

"It does." I nodded. "I should also warn you that what I'm about to ask could be dangerous for you, though I'm not quite sure how."

"You don't have to worry about me, Candace," he said. "I can take care of myself. What do you need me to do?"

"Follow me and I'll show you."

* * *

"Holy shit," Chet said moments later, his voice truly awed. We were standing in the doorway of my hidden office. He had approached the room cautiously. But I could see he understood its purpose at once.

"You really do it, don't you?" he said, and I could hear a tremor of excitement threading through his voice. "What happened New Year's wasn't a onetime deal. You really fight them."

More quickly now, he moved to the first of a series of cabinets with wide, shallow drawers. Their original purpose was to house architectural drawings. I had made some modifications. Chet slid the top one open, took in its contents. Silver stakes in an array of thicknesses and sizes. He picked one up, as if to test its weight in his hand, then turned toward me.

"You fight back," he corrected himself. "You take them out."

"Not all of them," I said. "Just the ones who feed on human blood. And before you get all starry-eyed, there haven't been all that many of those."

Chet closed his eyes, as if suddenly dizzy, then opened them again. "What can I do to help?"

"I want you to help me keep what's in this room safe," I said. "I may not be able to come back here for a while. I'm thinking you should take the lap-top and discs, the reference library, and any of the weapons you want."

Chet's head swiveled, his eyes fixed on my face. "Are you in some kind of trouble?"

I shook my head. "No. But there are some per-sonal matters I have to take care of that will take up a lot of time, keep me away from home. I don't want to run the risk of losing everything I've got here, Chet."

Whether Ash had been its impetus or not, I had worked hard for what this room contained, and what it represented. Power, knowledge. And I was not about to let it go to waste.

"Okay," Chet said slowly, his eyes still on my face. "I can understand that."

"Nobody else knows about what's here, Chet," I went on. "No one else even knows this room exists. Not Bibi, not Al. No one. That's the way it has to stay. If you take this on, you're on your own."

"Are you asking for my help or trying to scare me off?"

"Both."

"The answer is still yes," Chet said.

"I'm really glad to hear it. I owe you one."

"I should pull my car into the garage," Chet

said. "That way, we can load up without any prying eyes."

"That's a great idea," I said.

He tucked a silver stake into the pocket protector he always wore in his front shirt pocket.

"I'll go get the car."

Half an hour later, we were done. My reference books, laptop computer, and backup discs, along with the items from my weapons collection Chet had decided he didn't want to be without, had all been safely loaded into the trunk of his car. The books he would keep at his own apartment. After copying the discs, he would store the originals in a safe-deposit box. While I sealed off my office and locked up the house, Chet pulled back out onto the street, leaving the engine running as he got out of the car.

"You take care, Candace," he said as I unlocked my own driver's side door.

"I will," I said. I opened the door, then turned back to face him. It was almost noon now. The sun bright as a new penny in the cloudless Vegas sky. Beneath the palm of my hand, the metal of the doorjamb felt hot enough to burn.

"Thanks for everything, Chet. I really mean that."

"Hey," he said, reaching out suddenly. "It's all right. I mean, that's what friends are for."

"Thanks just the same," I said. "I'll be in touch."

I turned to climb into the car. Without warning, my stomach lurched. The pavement swooped upward. Hot-white spots danced before my eyes. If I hadn't been clutching the top of the door, chances are good I would have fallen.

"Whoa," Chet said, reaching out to steady me. "Are you all right? Jesus, Candace. Your skin is like ice."

"I'm fine," I said. "Forgot to eat breakfast, that's all. It's just low blood sugar. Nothing to worry about."

Clenching my stomach muscles against the nausea sweeping through me, I climbed into my car.

"You sure you're okay to drive?" Chet insisted. "I could drop you wherever you need to go. You could come back for your car when you're feeling better."

"I'm fine," I said, summoning a smile. "Don't worry."

"But I'm really good at that," he protested.

"I can see that," I said. "Now stop. Go home. And thanks again. I really, really mean that."

Before he could get another word in, I put the key in the ignition, turned it, and brought the car to life. Chet stepped back as I put the car in gear and drove off. Just before I turned the corner, I glanced back in the rearview mirror. He was still standing in the street outside my house. Hands on hips, a puzzled, slightly worried expression on his face.

I turned the corner, and he was lost to sight.

Eight

By the time I reached Ash's house, my hands were shaking. My stomach was tied in knots. Even with my sunglasses on, the glare of the sun seemed to cut across my vision like a sword. I pulled into the driveway and turned off the engine. Before I had the car door halfway open, Ash was there, striding quickly toward me down the front walk. He caught my hand in his, slowly but firmly drawing me out of the car, then ushered me into the house. The second I felt its cool darkness envelop me, I began to feel better.

Ash pulled me into his arms. "I was worried about you," he murmured. "Where have you been? Why did you go out? You know it's not good for you, Candace."

"*You* went out," I managed. "Last night."

His arms tightened for a moment. I thought I could feel him consciously relax them.

"Is that what this is? Tit for tat?"

I gave a sigh. "Of course not. You have things to

take care of. So do I. Now, I've done it. Now, I'm home."

He stepped back, slid a hand down my arm to hold mine, tugged me farther into the house.

"Where are we going?" I asked.

He reached to tilt my face toward him. "You should feed, Candace," he said quietly.

"No," I said at once, jerking my head back, out of his grasp. "Do you hear me, Ash? *No.* It's taking a toll on you—don't think I can't tell. And I'm tired of being run by this. I want, I *need,* to take back some control."

"That's not the way, Candace," Ash said simply. "No vampire can entirely control the need for blood. It's like human beings and oxygen. It's what we need to survive."

"Well, I don't need it right now."

I moved away then, with no clear sense of where I wanted to go. My body felt thick and sluggish, achy. My eyes were dry, my eyelids moving across them like sandpaper. I traveled no more than half a dozen steps before I swayed on my feet. I heard Ash move then, felt him lift me into his arms. I gripped him, tightly.

"We're not going to have a repeat performance of yesterday," I said. "I'm not going to behave like an animal. Not again."

"Be quiet, Candace," Ash said, but there was no

heat in his voice. Swiftly, he began to move through the house. With a dim sense of surprise, I realized just how large it was, and how little of it I had taken the time to explore. All my time had been spent with Ash, in the bedroom we shared or out in the world I was learning how to inhabit. Now, room after room seemed to unfold around me like some intricate Chinese puzzle box.

Ash reached a door, came to a stop. Since his arms were full of me, I leaned down to turn the knob. The door swung silently back, and I felt a current of soft, moist air flow across my face. In front of us, a flight of stairs plunged down. Ash took them, moving on sure feet in the semidarkness. The moisture in the air increased as we went lower. It smelled green, like growing things. I thought I heard the splash of water. I wasn't sure if it was my exhausted senses or the lack of light, but it felt like a long way down.

"Where are we going?" I inquired.

"Someplace I think you'll like."

We reached the bottom of the stairs. Ash set me on my feet, holding me close, then reached to one side. Slowly, as if he was twisting a dimmer switch, the room around us came to life. Before us was a deep pool, so large I couldn't see its outer edges. They extended into the soft, moist darkness. But the corners I could see were lush with plants. Vines hung down from the ceiling. I thought I recognized the thick, broad leaves of banana trees. A vivid splash of color that could only be some kind of orchid. *It's a tropical paradise,* I thought. Transported to the Las Vegas desert, then hidden underground like buried treasure.

"The previous owner came from Hawaii," Ash explained quietly. "This is the reason I bought this particular house. I think you'll find this place will soothe you, Candace. It always does me."

"Thank you," I said.

"Oh, don't thank me yet," Ash replied gravely. "It's way too soon for that."

For the first time in what felt like days, I smiled. Ash was right. This place did make me feel better, even if I wasn't quite sure why. Perhaps it was the moisture in the air, which seemed to give a strange, nurturing quality to the darkness, but I could feel my body's discomfort begin to ease. The presence of water somehow drawing out the teeth of my terrible need.

"What do you mean by that?" I asked.

Ash leaned down, kissed me gently. "Let's find out."

Hand in hand, we moved toward the water. But when I would have knelt to remove my shoes, I suddenly found that Ash was already kneeling before me. Easing my feet from my well-worn boots. He was already barefoot, I noticed.

With the same deliberation, he curled his fingers beneath the edge of my T-shirt then drew it up and off. I felt a different stir of need now, both more and less complicated than my need for blood.

His fingers traced my bra straps to the clasp in front, and I arched back as his quick hands freed my breasts to cup them. He bent his head, tongue dancing across one nipple as he pulled my breast deep inside his mouth. I felt both harden in a swift, hard jolt of want.

"Ash," I gasped out.

I reached for his head, to urge his mouth to mine. He rolled his head within my grasp, as if to shake it loose, then turned his attention to my other breast. One arm circled my back like a band, holding me to him, holding me up.

"Slowly, Candace," he whispered. "Let me taste you."

I let my head fall back as Ash's mouth continued its explorations. He was moving languidly now, openmouthed across my flesh. Teeth scraping ever so slightly, his tongue swirling in great, slow strokes. I felt his hand move to the fastenings of my jeans, ease them open to slide the denim down. His mouth followed the path of his hands. Abruptly dizzy, I braced myself on his shoulders as he lifted first one leg, then the other, to draw the jeans away. His hands kneading my ass, gently, insistently. His mouth dancing across my belly, then moving inexorably down. The only thing between us was a thin triangle of silk. The second I felt Ash press his mouth against it, I cried out.

He hooked a single finger into the waistband of the silk, then tugged it down. It skimmed down the length of my legs with a whisper. Ash's mouth returned to the juncture of my thighs. As if in slow motion, I lifted one leg to step out of the panties. Ash caught my leg behind the knee, nestling it against his shoulder, broadening my stance even as he steadied me. I felt his tongue flick out. Dancing across my clit, then settling in to stroke. Moaning now, I threw my head back, taut breasts thrusting up. I ran my hands across them, feeling the hard roll of my own nipples beneath my flat palms, and heard Ash make a sound of approval, low in his throat.

He released my leg, and I swayed on my feet. Quickly, Ash stood, then lifted me up into his arms. I put my own around his neck, leaned down, and ran my tongue along the length of his jaw, nipped with my teeth against his mouth. I felt it curve a fraction of a second before it opened to my insistent probing. Ash's tongue met mine in a long, slow glide. The taste was tangy, ever so slightly exotic.

That is my taste, I thought.

He began to walk then, taking us both closer to the pool. When we reached it, he set me down. I felt warm water lap around my ankles, smooth and thick, like satin. I felt with my foot to make sure of the bottom, then stepped farther into the water, saw Ash's flicker of surprise.

Thought I'd just rip that shirt right off you, didn't you? I thought, and smiled. Though, in all fairness, I did have something of a track record in that department. I continued moving backward. The water was at the top of my knees now. I let it reach the tops of my thighs before I spoke.

"Since you're so very good with clothes," I said. "I think you should be the one to handle your own. You said you preferred not to rush? That's all right. You can take your time." I saw a flash of understanding, of appreciation, leap into his face. "Feel free to start whenever, and wherever, you'd like," I went on. "I'm sure I can find some way to amuse myself in the meantime."

I ran my hands down the sides of my body till they plunged into the water. Then, leaving one beneath the surface, I slicked the other back up the front. I cupped one breast, thrusting the nipple toward him, as if in silent promise of reward. His eyes never leaving mine, Ash's fingers moved to the buttons on his shirt cuffs. He loosed them, then slid the shirt's front buttons from their buttonholes. He shrugged the shirt off his shoulders and let it fall to the ground. Beneath the shirt, his skin was bare. The finely wrought muscles of his pale chest glowed like alabaster in the dim light.

I released my breast to slide my hand up my neck, exposing it as I lifted up my hair. I eased myself into the water until it reached my chin, then stood up suddenly, bringing the hand in the water up to join the other at the back of my head. Water sluiced down. At the sudden change in temperature, I felt my breasts tighten even more. Ash's fingers were moving quickly now. Flicking open the button on his pants then easing down the zipper of his fly. With a sudden, almost brutal gesture, he pushed both his pants and underwear down, then stepped out of them. His cock leaped out, jutting proudly from his body, thick and long.

"I thought you wanted to go slow," I said.

"I changed my mind."

Ash made a sudden lunge, but I was ready for him. It was the obvious move, after all. Pushing backward out of range with a great whoosh of water, laughing as I heard him plunge in after me. I felt his fingers tangle with my toes. I kicked, sending water into his face, then stroked away. But Ash was quick. I felt one hand close around my ankle as, with a great yank, he pulled me toward him. I had time for one shout of laughter before the water closed over my head.

I let the momentum of Ash's gesture pull me through the water, down along the length of his body. I reached out to grasp his ass with both hands, gripped it tightly to stop my movement, then ran my tongue up along the length of his cock. His body gave a jerk.

I grinned then, reveling in my own power. There were other aspects of our relationship where Ash was clearly the stronger. It had been that way from the very first moment we met. But when our bodies met in passion, we were equally matched in the strength of our desire. I made a second sweep up the length of his cock, scraping gently with my teeth this time, then took it into my mouth. I felt his body jerk again, his fingers reach to tangle in my hair as it spread out around my head beneath the water.

I felt a great jolt of unexpected joy, of laughter, surge inside my chest. If I were human, I'd be giving serious consideration to a breath of air right about now. Instead, I was entirely free to devote my attentions to my lover.

Ash's hands were more insistent now, urging my head upward. After making very sure he knew what he'd be missing, I released my hold, slithered upward along his body, bursting through to the surface in a spray of water. I had time enough to shake the hair back from my face before Ash's mouth found mine. Tongue jutting in to claim possession. His hands swept up my body, molding mine to his. I felt them reach my ass. He squeezed urgently then lifted me up. I spread my legs, wrapping them around his waist, pressing my crotch against his cock but refusing to take him inside. It seemed I wasn't quite ready to give up the sensation of being the one in control.

Ash's mouth left mine to roam across my face and bite the soft flesh of one earlobe.

"You're going to make me crazy," he said.

"Turnabout is fair play," I responded. Over his shoulder, on the edge of the pool, I caught a glimpse of a broad, low shelf, bordered by lush plant fronds. *Perfect*, I thought. I turned my head, so that our lips met again, dancing across his, teasing with my teeth and tongue. "Back up."

"Hmmm?" Ash murmured. Without warning, he opened his mouth and caught my lips between his teeth, flicking across them with his tongue. I gasped, and twisted, managing to break free enough to capture his lower lip between my teeth.

Hungry. I am so hungry for you, I thought. "Ash," I said again, more urgently this time. "Back up."

He closed his eyes, as if to better sense where he

was going. Our mouths still busy together, Ash began to back slowly through the water, our passage providing exquisite friction against my open thighs. Slowly, we made our way to the far side of the pool. The moment Ash felt the shelf against the back of his legs, he stopped. I dropped my legs, placing my feet against the edge of the shelf, and pushed myself away from his body. Ash opened his eyes. I saw the silver glitter of them, like fireflies in the dim light. His hands dropped to my ass, positioning me, urgently.

I shook my head. "No. Not yet. There's something else I want."

"Then take it," Ash said.

I pushed again, the momentum carrying me away from his body, and this time, Ash let me go. I stood for a moment, watching him, the water lapping just below his waist. The tip of his cock, just below the waterline. My eyes on his, I moved toward him. Hands flat against his chest, I applied pressure until he eased down onto the shelf. His cock rose up, out of the water. I urged him back farther still, so that he lay spread-eagled, and felt a surge of outrageous desire. Never had I seen Ash so exposed.

I knelt down facing him, my own body in the water. Again, I ran my tongue up along the length of Ash's cock, watched the way it pulsed and shuddered. So many tastes and textures, all so different from my own. The blunt head of his penis with its texture like velvet, the taut, thick shaft thrusting up from the firm, round balls.

Mine, I thought. *Mine to love. Mine to control.*

I closed my wet hands around Ash's cock, squeezing and releasing again and again. I flicked my tongue, swirling and dancing it around his head, until I heard him groan. Ash had wanted me to feed, and now I did. Not on his blood, but on his need, his desire. The passion he felt for me, and me alone. Until I felt his body tremble with his effort to hold himself back.

No, I thought. *Not this time.*

I had feasted on Ash like an animal, driven only by need, without conscious thought. Now, I would make him do the same. With my tongue, with my mouth, with my body, I would make him lose control. I would make him feed his desire.

I let my mouth leave his cock, moving downward to bite the sensitive skin on the inside of his thighs. Instinctively, he moved to close his legs. I slid down beneath the surface of the water then stroked backward, away from the shelf. Ash followed at once, body sluicing into the water. He reached for me. I eluded his grasp, rolling over onto my stomach as I propelled myself forward.

You want me? I thought. *Come and get me. Come for me.*

Without warning, the opposite edge of the pool loomed into view. I shot toward it, intending to reach it, then bank away. But Ash was too quick for me. Trailing a stream of bubbles, he shot past me. I backstroked, trying to slow my momentum, and felt one hand grasp me around the elbow. Ash pulled me to him with a jerk. I yanked back, against his hold, but he was simply too strong. Our bodies crashed together. Ash bowed me back, pulling one breast deep inside his mouth. I twisted against him, as if trying to get away, though we both knew, full well, what this game was. Together, we broke the surface of the water in a cascade of water.

My legs were around Ash's waist again, now. His hands at my back, steadying me as his ravenous mouth moved from one breast to the other. I braced my legs against the edge of the pool, lowered myself until I felt the blunt tip of Ash's cock at the entrance to my body. I let it penetrate, then pulled myself up. A second, and then a third time, taking him in a little deeper each time I returned, I teased him, teased us both, until I began to feel my own game begin to catch up with me. There was only one thing that could feed the hunger that drove me now: Ash, inside my body.

"Do it, Ash," I panted. "Do it. Fuck me."

He made a sound then that I cannot describe. A sound so pure and elemental, I felt my whole body tighten in response. I felt the world spin, and belatedly realized we had turned around. Ash took several churning steps through the water, then hoisted me up and out, onto a shelf I hadn't even noticed, turning my body so that my back was to him. I understood what he wanted at once. Even as I felt his hands upon my ass, I was shifting to my knees, opening my body to him, legs braced, pelvis tilted up. I felt his hands slide around to seize my breasts, capturing the nipples between his fingers and squeezing tightly.

"Now," I said. "Ash, *now.*"

His hands dropped to steady my hips, and then his body was surging forward. Filling me in a single stroke, potent, powerful. I made a sound of my own then lowered my head down onto my hands, tilted my ass up higher, pushed back hard. I heard him give a grunt as he pulled his cock back, then drove forward once more. He wrapped a hand around my belly to hold me still as he set a hard, fast rhythm. Neither of us was going to last long. We both needed too much. The fingers of his free hand moved between my thighs even as the force of his thrusts drove the water against my clit. I felt time stretch, suspend, and, at long last, stop.

For an infinitesimal second, my body hung in the balance. Senses crying out for release even as they begged for more. *No!* I thought. I dug my fingernails into my own skin in a desperate attempt to hold on to my passion. I would not be first, not this time. I would see this game that I had started through to its conclusion. This time, it would be Ash who lost control. I threw back my head and screamed aloud, and as I did, Ash's tempo increased. Primal as a heartbeat.

"Candace," he said. "For the love of God."

And I knew that I had won.

I felt him go absolutely still then, his cock rock-hard within my body, his entire body straining as it reached for desire's prize. I clenched my muscles, as if determined to hold him there forever. Knew the second he came undone. He called out, even as his body began to buck and plunge. Sobbing now, glorying in Ash's release, I let myself go, let his passion carry me along. The orgasm rolled through me like a shimmering wave, rolling me beneath it even as it bore me up upon its crest, until the world was gone. There was no daylight world of humans, no shadowy vampire nights. There was only this blinding wave of passion that Ash and I created together. In a universe of uncertainties, this was the only thing that would last. This was the thing for which I would fight death itself.

As if from a great distance, I felt Ash ease out of my body, turn me gently so that I faced him, then slip back inside. My body quivered as it welcomed him back. Ash leaned down, kissed my eyelids closed, then moved his tongue across them in a gesture that made my throat ache, it felt so sweet.

"I love you, Candace Steele," he said.

I opened my eyes, gazed upward. Ash's hair, always slightly too long, dripped down into his eyes. I reached to push it back, let my fingers linger over the contours of his face, as if by doing so I could help commit it to memory.

"I love you, Ashford Donahue the third," I replied. Then an odd thought occurred to me. "If we had a son, would he be Ashford Donahue the fourth?"

"God forbid," Ash said. He was silent for a moment. Our mutual passion well and truly spent, I could feel his body begin to soften, though it stayed within my own. "I'm sorry," he said.

"For what?"

He was silent for a moment. "For all the things we'll never have, I guess," he said at last. "I would have liked to give you a child."

I reached up, brought his mouth to mine for a long, slow kiss, even as I felt the tears build at the back of my eyes. He nestled his face in the crook of my neck.

"Jesus, Ash," I said.

"I know," he said. He pressed a kiss into the hollow of my throat. "I know. I have learned to live without regret. If I hadn't, I would have gone mad long ago. Maybe that's why I love you so much. You show me so many possibilities, Candace, even if they're ones I know I am denied."

"I don't know what to say to you," I confessed. "I wish I did but I don't."

A child, I thought. *Our child.* If Ash were like other men, such a thing might have been possible. And if he were, would I love him as much?

He raised his head then, and his silver eyes looked down. Straight and direct, never more beautiful than in this moment.

"You can tell me that you love me," he said.

"I do love you. I will never stop loving you."

"Then I am content," he said. He smiled suddenly and flicked a finger down my nose. "And I'm getting you out of this water before we both turn into prunes."

"I should hope so," I said, sliding into the teasing in spite of the ache at the back of my throat. "If there's one thing I can't stand, it's a pruney vampire."

Hand in hand, we left the pool behind.

Several hours later, as the cool of the evening settled over the city, I perched on a tall stool in the kitchen, watching as Ash deftly dressed a salad. *What is it about passion that inspires domesticity?* I suddenly wondered. Was it the desire to further claim one's mate? To feed one's love in all the ways that are possible? I took a sip of deep-red wine, savoring its earthy taste. Neither Ash nor I actually needed the food he was preparing, not in the way we had when we were altogether human. It would not truly sustain us. But there was still something about the ritual of food preparation that felt intimate, as if it were a gift. I took a second sip, watching as Ash unwrapped two enormous steaks.

"Ash," I said. "How long have you been a vampire?"

He paused in the act of shaking seasonings onto the steaks. "What makes you ask that all of a sudden?"

"It's not particularly sudden," I said. "I guess I've always wanted to know. It never seemed quite right to ask before." I took another sip of wine. "I'll withdraw the question if you like."

He shook his head, as if to clear it. "No. I was created in the time of the earthquake."

I set the wineglass down on the counter with a sharp *click,* certain I must have misunderstood.

"The San Francisco earthquake," I said. A statement, not a question.

Ash nodded.

"Not Loma Prieta," I persevered. "The—what do they call it . . . the other one?"

"The great earthquake," Ash said quietly. "And yes, I do mean that."

"But that was . . ." I began. With a quick gesture, Ash slapped the steaks onto the stovetop grill, cutting me off. Not that I would have been able to get another word out, anyhow. My throat had gone abruptly thick, as if all my questions were jockeying for position at once.

The meat hit the metal with a sharp, hot sizzle. Ash left them for the amount of time it took him to reach for a pair of tongs. He flipped the steaks, slid a pair of dinner plates into position beside the grill, then lifted the steaks off. It pretty much gave a whole new definition to the term *rare*. He moved to the counter where I sat motionless upon my stool and plunked the plates down. Only when he was seated, facing me, did he speak.

"Nineteen aught six," he said.

I felt dizzy. 1906. The man I loved was more than a hundred years old. Had been a vampire for more than a hundred years, I silently corrected myself. Ash had stopped counting his age in human years long before I was born.

"Those days were . . . chaos," he went on quietly. He cut a slice of steak, its interior bright with blood, and held it out to me. "Eat this, Candace," he said.

I did as he requested, feeling the texture of the meat inside my mouth, the sensuous feel of the juice and blood slipping down the back of my throat.

"Days of earth and water, fire and blood. I have never seen their like again, nor do I want to. Even the one who made me was shaken by them. I think that's why she created me, instead of just feeding then leaving me to die. Even those who dwell in the darkness could not bear the terror of those days."

She, I thought, then realized I wasn't altogether surprised. Another man might have simply taken Ash when he was weak then walked away. But a woman would not have wanted to discard him. A woman would have wanted to keep him with her.

"Did you come to love her?"

"No," Ash said quickly, shaking his head. "There was never any question of that. But I did come to feel a sense of gratitude." His mouth quirked up. "After I got over the initial shock. She gave me what so many others lost during those terrible days: the means to survive."

He lifted his gaze from his plate, at last, and met mine. "But I don't look back, Candace. I never have. Those days are over. It's what's coming next that interests me. What I want, only the future holds."

"And what is that?" I whispered, though I had a feeling I knew quite well.

"A life with you," Ash said simply, "if you'll allow me to use the word *life*. You are the first person I have loved in more than a hundred years, Candace. I thought I had forgotten how to love. I know I had forgotten why. You brought color back into my world. I am not ever going to let you go."

"Ash," I said. "I . . ."

A sound cut through the air of the kitchen, sharp and sudden as the thrust of a knife.

"That's my cell phone," I said. My shoulder bag was sitting on a table near the front door.

"Let it go," Ash said, his tone slightly impatient. As if it had heard him, as suddenly as it had sounded, the phone cut off. I cut a slice of my own meat, and heard the phone sound again. I dropped the knife and fork onto my plate, hopped off the stool, and rushed to the front hall.

"For crying out loud, Candace," Ash called out.

"It's Bibi," I called back. "We have this code. A call, a hang up, and a call back means there's something wrong."

And it has to be bad, I thought as I reached my

shoulder bag and pulled it open to dig out my cell phone. I located the phone, flipped it open.

"I'm here," I said.

"Candace," Bibi said my name on a sob. "You have to . . . there's something . . ."

"Where are you?" I broke in, but Bibi was sobbing in earnest now. Great choking gasps. The sound of them wrenched my heart. "Bibi," I said, raising my voice. "I need you to keep it together. Take a deep breath and tell me where you are."

I heard her breath shudder in then out. "Penthouse," she said. "I'm at the penthouse."

"I'm on my way," I said. "I'm coming, do you hear me? Whatever this is, it will be all right."

She made a strangled sound, a laugh and a sob at once. "Say that again when you get here," she said. Then, as if that complete sentence had exhausted her strength, she ended the call. I snapped the phone shut, tossed it back into the bag, then pulled the bag up onto my shoulder. I turned. During my brief conversation, Ash had followed me out into the entry hall.

"Bibi needs me," I said. "I have to go."

"I'll drive you," he said at once.

I shook my head. "No. Not that I don't appreciate it, but you're not exactly her favorite person at the moment." *Or any moment,* I thought. "I'm sorry but your coming along for the ride won't help things. I couldn't even get a straight answer about what's wrong."

"I didn't say I would come along for the ride," Ash said, and I could tell by the tone of his voice that he was fighting to keep it even. "I said that I would drive you to wherever it is you're going. I'm not letting you go into unknown danger alone, Candace. It's as simple as that."

He moved past me, pulled the door open with a yank. "So let me say it again, I'll drive."

"Thank you very much," I said. I stomped past him. He slammed the door behind us. I got halfway down the walk, then stopped, turning back so suddenly Ash crashed right into me. He reached to steady us both, his hands gripping my elbows, tightly.

"I don't know what's happening," I said again. "I don't want to fight. She's my best friend, Ash. I have to do this. I have to try and help."

He leaned down, pressed a hard kiss to my mouth. "I know you do," he said. "It's one of the reasons why I love you. And if you tell me one more time that I make it hard for you to stay mad at me, the deal's off."

"In that case, I hate your fucking guts," I said.

Ash gave a wolfish grin, dropped a second kiss on my mouth.

"Outstanding," he said. "Now tell me where we're going."

I turned toward the street then. Together, the two of us hurried toward the car.

"To the Scheherazade," I said. "Randolph Glass's penthouse."

Nine

The second Ash pulled up at the curb outside the Sher, I was out of the car. We had agreed he would park and wait for me downstairs. I had no idea how long I would be. I had no idea what was going on. My tension and fears had only increased on the drive into town. Ash and I hadn't spoken much, but he had held my hand, silently offering support.

"Don't forget . . ." Ash began as he brought the car to a halt. But I already had the car door open, one foot planted firmly on the sidewalk. I levered myself out of the car, dashed the few steps to the Sher. With a blast of cold air, the automatic doors slid open as I approached. I barreled through the doorway then stopped as the wave of human experience crashed into me, sharp and vicious as a sucker punch.

Don't forget to take a moment to prepare yourself, Candace, I thought, mentally finishing the sentence I hadn't let Ash complete. Wrapped in my fears for Bibi, I had not taken time to remember to center myself, to inhabit the place I had discovered before, the one I now secretly referred to as the "undead zone." The place where my vampire powers would buffer me from human experience rather than making me a conduit for them.

I reached inward, searching for the place that would steady me, felt a sudden hand on my elbow, and jumped a good half mile. The fact that I realized who it was even as I overreacted didn't help any.

"About that nickname I gave you," Al Manelli said, dropping my elbow as I spun around.

"I'm changing it," I snapped. "As of this moment, it's Nerves of Jell-O. How's Bibi? Have you seen her? What the hell is going on?"

"I don't know," Al said, not specifying whether he was answering my first question or my last one. He took my elbow once again and began to pilot me through the crowd, toward the private elevator that would take us to Randolph Glass's penthouse. "All I know is that there's been an attack on Randolph."

I had a sick feeling in the pit of my stomach, one that even the undead zone couldn't protect me from.

"What kind of attack?"

Al ran his key card down the slot to activate the elevator. The security system beeped, just once, and the elevator doors slid open. In tandem, Al and I stepped inside, turning to face them as they whispered closed.

Al ran a hand across his face, and I realized in that moment just how rattled he was. "I'm not altogether sure," Al admitted as the elevator began to rise. "All I know is that it looks pretty bad, and that it happened in the penthouse. The paramedics are prepping him for transport now."

"Okay, wait a minute," I said. "He was attacked *in* the penthouse?"

No wonder Al is so shocked. Randolph's penthouse has security that would make the president green with envy. Personally, I would have given better odds on a successful break-in at Fort Knox.

Al nodded, his expression grim. "Bibi was the one who found him. They were supposed to have dinner together, before her first show. She walked through the door and—"

"What about the security tapes?" I broke in.

"Chet's looking at them now," Al responded, his tone growing even darker. "Apparently, they're not telling him much."

Nothing on the security tapes. That fact told me pretty much all I needed to know. Randolph had been attacked in the most secure location in the entire casino complex: his own penthouse. If the security tapes didn't show anyone entering or leaving by the private elevator . . .

Okay, Candace. Slow down. Don't make any assumptions, I warned myself. The situation seemed more than bad enough without my leaping to conclusions about it. If what I suspected, what I feared, was true, I would be able to see for myself, soon enough.

The elevator reached the penthouse, and the doors slid open. Al stepped off first. I took a moment to steady myself, and followed. I took about five steps then stopped, stock-still.

He hadn't told me about the blood.

It was everywhere, assaulting my senses, a sledgehammer and a siren's call, all at once. A pool of it spread across the floor on the far side of the room where, beneath an enormous bank of picture windows, a team of paramedics worked to keep Randolph Glass alive. They were clustered so tightly around him, only his legs were visible to me, strangely loose and useless in their elegant slacks. His feet were turned out at odd angles to his body. A soughing sound filled my ears, the hoarse, desperate passage of air in and out of a windpipe that was struggling to perform its function. *Randolph's breathing,* I thought. I took two stumbling steps forward then forced myself across the room to gaze down over the closest paramedic's shoulder.

Someone had done their best to rip out Randolph Glass's throat.

The paramedic glanced back, concern for his patient battling with irritation over the potential interruption.

"Ma'am," he said, in a tight, hard voice. "I'm going to have to ask you to step back."

I stayed right where I was. I had no doubt. *A vampire had attacked Randolph.*

As if from a distance, I realized the paramedic had risen to his feet. "Step back," he commanded sharply. "Step back right now!"

He laid a hand on my arm to force me away and, as if the undead zone I inhabited were a pane of glass, I felt my self-control splinter into a thousand knife-edged shards. My senses stripped bare in a roomful of human desperation. Human pain, fear, and blood. There was so much blood.

And I wanted it. Every single drop.

I lashed out, knocking the paramedic's hand from my arm. "Take your goddamn hands off me," I choked out. I could hear the blood sing inside his veins, hear the way Randolph's heart pounded, desperate to keep on going. The desire, the *need* to feed became a red-hot knife twisting in the center of my gut. The room swam before my eyes.

"Candace!" Bibi's voice rang out.

I turned my head toward the sound and saw her burst through the archway that led to the inner rooms of the penthouse. Bibi's face was streaked with tears. Her skin was red and splotchy. I could hear her blood shrieking through her veins. The desperate, anxious beating of her heart. And I knew, in that moment, what would happen next.

She was going to touch me.

Throw her arms around my neck, certain I would hold her, offer this basic, human comfort, one friend to another. But I also knew that if I let Bibi, if I let any human being, touch me now, I would lose control, push the paramedics aside, kneel down beside Randolph Glass, and finish the job the first vampire had begun. No power on earth would be able to stop me. I would not be able to stop myself.

"Don't!" I said, lifting my hands as if to block her onward rush. *"Bibi, don't touch me."*

At the sound of my voice, Bibi froze, her hands extended in front of her, as if anticipating our embrace. For a moment out of time, we stared at each other. I saw the hope of comfort fade from her eyes to be replaced with a pained confusion, wounded disappointment. Randolph's labored breathing was loud in the room.

"I'm sorry, but I have to go," I said. "Please, don't try and stop me."

"Candace . . . ," Bibi said once more, and I thought the sound might break my heart.

Hugging my arms close to my body, I made a dash for the elevator. The doors were closed.

"Open the doors, Al," I barked. He took a step toward me. I took a step away. *"Just open the fucking elevator doors."*

His face set, eyes narrowed, Al stepped to the control panel, slid his key card along the slot. The elevator doors parted immediately. I stepped between them, pivoted so that I faced the room.

"For God's sake, Nerves," Al began. He stuck one foot between the doors.

"Don't," I said. "Just don't, Al. I'm sorry. I'm so sorry." I kept my eyes on him. I could not look at Bibi anymore. Couldn't bear the expression in her eyes. The shock that I was running out on her. I hoped she would never have to know why.

"This isn't over," Al Manelli said.

I could feel hysteria, rising within me, inexorable as a tide. My vision was red now. Red with the blood I wanted so desperately, the need I wanted, so desperately, to deny.

"Don't you think I know that?" I shouted. "If I could make another choice, I would. Now move your foot before I break every bone in it."

"Do it, Al," I heard Bibi's voice say. "She doesn't want to be here. Let her go."

Al moved then, sliding his foot back. The last thing I saw before the elevator doors hid the room from view were the tears streaming silently down Bibi's face.

I hit the lobby at a dead run. Forcing my way through the crowded casino, desperate to get out, into the open air. Even a crowded sidewalk would be better than being indoors.

Hurry, hurry, hurry, my mind chanted. My body, one enormous mass of need now. I pressed a hand to my mouth, bit deep into my own flesh as I hurtled toward the front doors and freedom. *Don't give in,* I thought. *Do whatever it takes to beat back the bloodlust.*

I could see the doors now. One last row of slot machines between me and the exit. There was a sudden blast of light and sound as the very last machine in the row hit the jackpot, began to pay out. The guy before it jumped up, waved a cowboy hat in the air, then threw his arms around the closest body. Bad luck on all counts that it was mine. I jerked away, one elbow flying up to catch him squarely in the nose. His howls of delight turning to a wail of outrage, he let go. Blood streamed down his face, and I knew that I was lost. That I had brought about my own downfall.

He stumbled backward, eyes wide with pain. I moved toward him, each step steady and inevitable, all thought gone, knowing only that I wanted and would have his blood. Then strong arms grabbed me from behind. Closing around me like iron bands. I felt myself being lifted, spun around, and carried at breakneck speed through the Sher's front doors and out onto the sidewalk. Dimly, the corner of my mind still capable of rational thought realized I wasn't fighting my captor.

"Ash," I gasped out.

"Just shut the fuck up." We reached the edge of the building. Ash took the corner fast, propelled us halfway along it before he set me down. Instantly, he spun me to face him, pinning me against the side of the building as if he was afraid I would try to bolt. "What the hell?"

"I'm sorry," I choked out. "I didn't mean to. I couldn't help—" I closed my eyes, wanting to pull myself together, then wrenched them open again. Inside my closed eyelids, as if engraved there forever, were images of Randolph Glass lying in a pool of his own blood.

Ash reached to cradle my face between his hands, his touch more gentle now. "Tell me, Candace," he said. "Take your time. Go slow."

"Randolph. It was Randolph," I said. "Something attacked him, in the penthouse."

"What do you mean some*thing*?" Ash asked at once.

My body had begun to tremble now, as if in shock. "There's nothing on the security tapes," I said. "I— It— His throat." I gave a sob then, and Ash folded me into his arms. "Blood, Ash. There was so much blood. I wanted it so much."

"We need to get you out of here," he said, his tone gentle and urgent all at once. "Let me take you home. You need to feed on me, Candace. I know you're trying to be strong, but you're fighting the wrong battle, one you can't win. *You have to feed, and feed now.* It's the only way to protect yourself."

I could feel a sickness rise within me then. A horror, a devastation of the soul. This is what being a vampire forever would mean. This elemental lust for blood. It would be with me, always. It would never let me go. The future Ash painted as so rosy, so filled with possibilities, was no more than eternal bloodlust. Eternal desperation. Eternal hunger with no chance of ever being truly satisfied.

I gathered my hands against his chest, then

pushed backward with all my might. Ash released me, staggering back, caught completely off guard.

"No!" I shouted, not caring if anyone saw or heard me. "I will not give in to any part of this. Do you hear me, Ash? *I won't give in. This isn't what I want.*"

He reached for me again, to soothe, to calm, or maybe to shake some sense into me. But by then I was running. Running fast, running away, with no thought or care of direction. The destination didn't matter. All I wanted was to outrun myself.

Some time later, I staggered up the front walk of my own house. My body covered with sweat, my muscles aching and sore. I had run all the way from the Sher, a distance of at least two miles. *Animal instincts. Gut instincts,* I thought. They always win out in the end. They never, ever lied. They were incapable of it. Gut instincts always told the truth.

And mine had brought me here, had brought me home.

Here, I would try to heal, try and start over. When in doubt, I had run from Ash, from all he represented, to the one place I trusted. The safe haven I had created for myself.

The front door was standing open.

No, no, no! I thought. With a cry of dismay, I forced my legs to carry me the last few steps, up onto the porch and into the entry hall. The house had been secure when Chet and I had left it . . . had it really been just that morning? My fingers fumbled against the light switch, snapped it on. I heard a voice make a wild exclamation of horror and denial, realized I had made the sound myself.

My living room looked as if it had been the victim of an attack by a team of manic set dressers for a TV cop show. *House ransacked,* the stage direction would have said. My furniture was overturned, the sofa cushions torn open, as if whoever had done this had used their teeth instead of a knife. Stuffing littered the floor. Every single vase had been shattered, every lamp overturned. Every single picture thrown down from the wall, glass from the frames glittered against my hardwood floors. I stepped forward, heard glass crunch, looked up. The decorative light fixture in my entry hall had been smashed to bits. It was a miracle the lightbulb had survived and still functioned.

My office, what about my office? I thought.

I was running again, through the ravaged rooms of my home. The door to my hidden office was ajar. I stepped inside and stopped, unable to believe what I was seeing. The destruction was almost pathological in its violence. My corkboard was torn to bits. The desk chair, dismembered, one of its legs used to help destroy the desk. The weapons Chet had decided not to take with him rested in heaps against the floorboards. As if they had been removed from the cabinet, flung against the walls in a blind rage, then allowed to rest where they had fallen. And the walls . . .

The walls were smeared with something thick and red, a substance I knew beyond a shadow of a doubt was not paint, but blood. Without warning, I doubled over, then collapsed to my hands and knees as my body screamed in agony, screamed in need, even as my mind fought to stay in control. I crawled forward a few scuttling steps, threw my head back and howled, nearly insane with pain and frustration.

I would not do what my body was demanding, crawl on my hands and knees like a beast to lick the blood off my own office walls.

Instead, still on my knees, I forced myself backward, out of the office. I pulled myself up on the doorjamb, triggered the mechanism. On silent hinges, the door to my secret office pivoted to a close, concealing the room from view once more. I sank down against its hard surface, pressing my face against my knees, desperately willing myself not to be sick, and heard the sirens. Somehow, the police had been summoned.

Pull yourself together, Candace. Pull yourself to-

gether, I chanted like a mantra in my mind. I was about to be face-to-face with living, breathing human beings whose only desire would be to offer me assistance. I didn't have to be cool, calm, and collected. No cop would expect that. But I did have to regain some semblance of control.

I bit down on my lip until I felt the skin part beneath my teeth. The taste of my own blood filled my mouth. Not what I wanted. Not what I needed, but it helped to steady me, somehow. Grateful for any small favor, I pulled myself to my feet, using the wall for support as the room swayed around me.

"Las Vegas police," I heard a voice call. "Anyone on the premises, identify yourself at once!"

"Here. I'm here!" I yelled.

A moment later, a young cop came into view, weapon drawn and at the ready.

"Ma'am," he said. "Please identify yourself."

"My name is Candace Steele," I said, keeping my voice as calm and steady as I could. "This is my house, and I'm alone."

"Candace, for the love of God," I heard a voice say.

And in that moment, I realized my knees were trembling. "Carl?" I said. *"Carl?"*

Detective Carl Hagen came into view. "It's all right, Officer," he said. "I'm acquainted with the victim. I'll take it from here."

The young cop stepped aside, holstering his gun. "I'll join my partner outside, do a quick sweep of the grounds."

"I appreciate that," Carl said.

The young cop disappeared from view, and the next moment, I was in Carl's arms.

"Easy, take it easy now, Candace," he said as my body began to shudder and sob. He let me get it out for a few moments then eased back to tilt up my face. "What's up with this, Steele?" he asked, his tone light though his eyes stayed watchful. "I thought you were big and bad and tough."

"So did I," I said. "Looks like we were both wrong. I'm just some puny, teary-eyed hormone factory in a skirt, just like every other female around. Dammit, Carl, look what the sonsofbitches did to my house!"

"I know," he said, easing me to his side so he could keep one arm around my shoulders. "I know. Let's go back into the living room where we can talk about this a little."

"Okay," I said. "But good luck finding a place to sit down."

I let him lead me, let myself lean against him. By the time we reached the living room, I almost had myself back together.

Carl and I perched on the edge of the ruined couch. "Don't take this the wrong way or anything," I said, "but what are you doing here, Carl? I seriously hope you haven't been demoted."

He smiled and shook his head. "Nope. One of your neighbors noticed your door standing open and reported a break-in. I heard the dispatch call. I'm . . ." He paused briefly, as if searching for the right word. "Aware of an incident earlier this evening, involving Randolph Glass." I nodded, to show I knew what he meant. "When I heard something was going down at your address, I thought I'd swing by, check it out myself."

"You mean you were worried about me," I said.

Carl regarded me thoughtfully, as if gauging my ability to take a joke. "Is that a crime?"

"No," I said, suddenly glad he'd made the attempt. Carl was good with people. We had been good together.

"You're sure you're not injured?" he asked.

I shook my head. "I'm not injured. Just freaked and pissed and tired. This whole thing sucks, Carl."

"Anything missing?"

I shook my head. "Not as far as I can tell." Abruptly, I felt tears threaten. Blinking to hold them back, I gave one of the ruined sofa cushions a jab with my toe. If I could stay mad, maybe I wouldn't give in to my sudden impulse to fling myself into Carl's arms and cry like a baby. "I can't promise for sure."

Carl was silent for a moment. I could feel his eyes studying my face. "They tore up the cushions pretty good, so I guess that means they got your stash of heroin."

It was the right, and the wrong, thing to say, all at once. I felt myself give a spurt of laughter in pure relief. The next second, the tears began to flow.

"Dammit!" I said. "Now look what you made me do. Dammit all straight to Hell, Carl."

"And back again." He pulled me toward him, tucking my head into the crook of his neck then wrapping his arms around me to hold on tight. "You know, sometimes it's better if you just cry and get it over with. Let it all out."

"I hate crying," I wailed, then laughed. If I'd ever sounded more petulant and ridiculous, I wasn't sure when.

"I know you do," Carl said soothingly. "I know it, sweetheart." He turned his head, pressed a quick kiss to my temple. "Do it anyhow."

"Being nice only makes things worse, you know."

"Well, damn," Carl said, entirely without heat. "And here I've left my billy club in the car."

I gave a watery laugh, leaned back so we were face-to-face.

"Carl, I . . ."

I saw the second the need flashed into his eyes. Potent, outrageous desire. Long withheld, maybe even long-suffering, but never entirely gone. His arms went rigid. I saw his eyes flick down to focus on my mouth.

"You *are* hurt," he said. "Candace, there's blood on your mouth."

I lifted it up. He brought his own down to meet it. *Sweet, sweet Jesus,* I thought. *But it feels good to kiss you, Carl.* Gently, at first, as if he feared to hurt me further, then with growing intensity, Carl's mouth moved against mine. Warm, vital, *alive.* I parted my lips, deepening the intimacy, and met the insistent probing of his tongue with my own. My hands curled against the base of his neck, where my head had rested just moments before. And I felt it then, the quickening beat of his pulse.

I groaned into Carl's open mouth, felt the instinctive tightening of his arms. *This, this is what I want,* I thought. *This sweetness. This strength.* I let my mouth leave his to wander across his jaw, down the side of his neck, until I could bracket that pulse with my open mouth. *This life,* I thought.

I put my tongue against Carl's neck. Felt the beat of his pulse, running high now. I heard his quick breathing, felt his hands at my breasts, and knew that I could take the thing I wanted and he would never know what hit him.

Blood. Now and forever, it is always about blood, I thought.

Although the sight of Randolph's blood had horrified me, here with Carl so close, so vulnerable, I was beginning to understand the power of the bloodlust. So many possibilities. So many desires, just waiting to be explored and satisfied. I could feed on Carl Hagen until my mind hazed high and hot and red. Strong and fit as he was, he would be powerless to fight, powerless to stop me. I began to writhe in his arms, and then, without warning, I heard Ash's voice.

"Candace!" he said, his voice like the crack of a whip.

Carl was on his feet in a blur of movement, pushing me backward, shielding my body with his own. His gun appearing in his hand as if by magic. Ash stood in the living room doorway, staring down the barrel of Carl's gun. Neither man moved a muscle.

"Carl," I finally said, as quietly and calmly as I could. "This is my friend, Ash. You remember, you met the other morning."

For an endless second, I thought Carl was going to deny the knowledge. Then, with the kind of quick, economical gesture I remembered so well, he pointed the gun away and holstered it.

"Of course I remember," he said. "Great to see you again, Donahue."

I might have laughed then, if the situation hadn't been so dire. I hadn't reminded Carl of Ash's last name; he'd remembered. Carl was a cop. Collecting and assembling details was what he did for a living, and I knew for a fact he was damned good at his job. Not only did he remember everything about that first meeting with Ash, he had probably run a background check on him.

"I was going to ask if you had a safe place to go tonight, Candace," Carl went on, the faintest tone of bitterness at the back of his voice. "I assume that's not necessary now."

"It's not," I said, rising to my feet. "I'm sorry, Carl."

He gave a mirthless laugh. "So am I. The trouble is, we've both been sorry before, haven't we, Steele? You want the truth? This is starting to bore the hell out of me."

He stepped toward the entry hall, and Ash moved aside to give him room.

"I'll check in with the patrol car," Carl went on. "You'll probably need to come down and file a report, but I think you're good to go for tonight. You need me for anything else, you know where to find me."

"I do," I said. "Thank you, Carl."

He started down the entryway only to turn back, his eyes on Ash this time.

"And I know where to find *you*," he said quietly. "You might want to remember that."

Then he turned and was gone. Ash and I stood, facing each other across my ruined living room.

Neither of us spoke. If Ash was jealous or angry, he kept his control. I flinched first.

"I have to get out of here," I said fiercely.

"Where do you want to go?"

"Someplace where I won't have to face what I'm not anymore."

Ash held out a hand. I stepped forward until I could place mine into it. Together, we went to find the other vampires.

Ten

Ash drove fast, the perfect match for my mood. I neither asked nor cared where we were going. My body was a raging fire of need. Desperate to satisfy some portion of the craving that rode me, I stroked him as we drove. Running my fingers along his shoulders, down one arm. Dancing my fingers across his legs to slide up and down the length of his crotch. Utterly without warning, he jerked the car to the curb, bringing it to a halt with a squeal of brakes. Then he captured my questing fingers in his.

"We're here," he said, his voice tight. "Get out of the car."

"Here" turned out to be a gorgeous, sprawling house, the dark windows facing the night like sightless eyes. But inside, I thought I caught a flicker of movement and of candlelight. Ash and I strode up the front walk, Ash knocked, the door opened. After a brief exchange, we were ushered inside. Ash had a low conversation with the young vampire who had admitted us, a male wearing a well-tailored suit, then beckoned me forward. Without a word, the vampire led us through the darkened house. We passed through what I assumed was the great room, until it opened into a series of vast, open chambers. Archways led to smaller rooms on the sides of these, but I could catch no more than glimpses of the activities in any of the rooms we passed.

We climbed a short flight of stairs, and our guide gestured to a room on the right. A filmy curtain of midnight blue hung across the doorway. I parted it and stepped inside.

Inside, the walls of the room were the same deep blue as the door hanging. A plush red carpet covered the floor. Cushions and low divans were scattered across it, most of them occupied. In the center was a couch of black velvet. On it, a vampire couple was making love.

The female sat astride the male, head thrown back, breasts straining forward as she rode him. Then a second male suddenly materialized behind her, his body rising up then flowing like liquid over the side of the couch. He knelt just behind her, knees on either side of the first male's legs, his hands reaching around to gather in the female's breasts, thumbs stroking. Instantly, her nipples formed hard, stiff peaks.

Ash and I stood silent, watching as the male behind her tilted her head back farther, claimed her mouth with his own. His hands stroked her breasts to the same rhythm her body had set, his tongue plunging in and out of her mouth. As the climax took her, I felt a hand slide along my arm. Startled, I cried out even as I felt my own body tighten in response. Standing before me, her hand grasping mine now, was a young female vampire. She was completely naked, her body glistening with scented oil.

They're all naked, I realized.

"You've come to join us," she said. "How nice." She cocked her head, as if considering. "But I think you have on too many clothes." She gave a laugh like the chime of silver bells. "I can help you with that, if you like," she offered.

She began to walk backward, toward the center of the room. The vampires on the couch, sated for the moment, lay in a tangle of arms and legs, but I saw the way they still stroked one another. As if this was only a lull, a quiet feeding of never-ending arousal. I let the female vampire pull me two steps, then four, then realized Ash was no longer behind me. I glanced back over my shoulder. He was still standing near the doorway, his silver eyes gleaming in the dim light.

"Don't worry," the female vampire said. "We won't forget about him."

Music began to whisper through the room, the lonely croon of a saxophone. The young vampire began to sway. She was holding both my hands now. Stepping in close, she eased them above my head, ever so slowly, as if testing how far I would go, then ran her open palms down the length of my uplifted arms. She slid one leg between my own, leaning in hard, pushing against my crotch. I pushed back, rubbing myself against her in time to the music. She made a sound of pleasure, deep in her throat.

With her hands, she reached for the loops of my jeans, used them to jerk my torso forward. The music was faster now, the two of us moving together like one body. From behind, I felt hands grasp the hem of my shirt, draw it up and off. I leaned back against the hard male body behind me, arms twisting back to wrap around his neck, as those same hands quickly moved to cup my breasts and release the front clasp of my bra.

As soon as my breasts were free, the female darted forward, flicking her tongue across my nipples. I gave a cry. The air in the room felt scorched with heat. And like my body, it throbbed.

Without warning, the female released me. I felt myself being spun around. She eased my arms down, slid the bra straps off them. Even as the male leaned down for an openmouthed kiss, I felt the female's tongue against my back, just between my shoulder blades, as her hands reached to stroke my breasts once more. Then her tongue began a long, slow glide straight down my spine, her hands moving lower at the same time as her mouth. With agile fingers, she made quick work of the fastenings of my jeans, then slid them down my legs, easing my panties down as well.

Before I could lift my leg to step out of the jeans, I felt myself being lifted, carried aloft on my back. There were more hands than I could count now. More open, seeking mouths. Stroking along my naked skin. Stoking the fire that burned inside my blood. I felt my legs being spread open, wide; knees slightly bent; pelvis tilted up, as if I were being offered as a sacrifice to some unseen god. And then I felt a tongue glide along my clit like a single slide of velvet. My body spasmed upward as I cried out.

And then, suddenly, Ash was there, naked, as I was. His silver eyes gleaming in the dim light, his cock jutting forward with the force of his own arousal. He reached for me, and the vampires who held me slid me forward into his arms, supporting me so that Ash filled me in one long, deep stroke. I moaned aloud. Wrapping my legs around his back,

I gave myself up completely to the feel of Ash's body, moving inside mine.

Faster and faster Ash moved within me. Deeper, harder. The vampires around us were all but frenzied now. Hands and mouths stroking against my skin, against Ash's, urging us both higher and higher.

I am flying, I thought.

"More, Ash," I gasped out. "I want more. It's not enough."

"Blood, Candace," I heard him answer. "The only thing more is blood."

He kissed me then, pulling my tongue deep inside his mouth. I felt the climax sweep through him as he bit down. Blood flooded both our mouths. I swallowed, felt its hot glide down my throat. And then I was coming on a wave of pleasure so great it seemed to me I left my body behind. It was only the passion that drove me. Passion for Ash, for all he offered. A passion as hot as fire, as red as blood.

With Ash's arms tight around me, I surrendered to all that drove us both, and lost myself.

When I came to myself again, I was lying on the floor. Alone, except for the female who had first enticed me. She was reclining on the velvet-covered sofa, still naked. Beside her, in a neat pile, were my clothes.

"Your companion is waiting for you," she said. "I told him I would bring you to him when you were ready." She gave me a smile full of sharp, white teeth. "Unless you'd like to stay a little longer, of course."

I got to my feet. "Thank you," I said. "But no."

I dressed quickly, aware of her eyes upon me the entire time.

"I'm ready," I said. "I'd like to go now."

She gave a disappointed look then a shrug. "Oh, very well."

She walked ahead of me, her body moving lithely, out of the room of midnight blue, down the short flight of stairs to the main level of the house, then toward the front door. Just as we reached the last of the great rooms, I heard a sudden cry. In the next moment, a young woman burst through a beaded curtain that covered one of the side arches. She staggered, then fell to her knees, blood streaming from a wound just above her left breast. A bite mark.

She's human, I realized.

Before I could even understand what I felt, the vampires in the room she had fled were upon her. Capturing her by her ankles, they dragged her backward into the room, the beaded curtain clacking like dead tree branches in the wind as she struggled. She splayed her hands flat against the hardwood floor, desperately trying to pull away. Her wild and terrified eyes looked straight up into mine.

"Please," she whispered. "Help me."

Then, with a yank that left a wide streak of blood on the floor, she was gone. From inside the room, there came one final shriek of horror and pain. Then nothing. No sound at all.

The young vampire who was my guide knelt down, ran her fingers through the blood on the floor, then brought them to her mouth. Then she grinned at me once more, her teeth stained bright red.

"They always taste better if they put up a fight."

And then, suddenly, Ash was there. I flung myself into his arms, pressing my head against his chest, shutting my eyes, and I let him lead me out into the night.

Eleven

Neither Ash nor I spoke as he piloted the Mercedes through the city toward his house. I leaned my head back against the headrest, listening to the way the engine purred, feeling the way the tires gripped the road. And slowly, as if Ash had created a cocoon, a cone of healing quiet, I realized the horrible need that had driven me since I had stepped out of the elevator into Randolph Glass's penthouse was altogether gone. But in its aftermath was the truth I had tried so desperately to stave off.

"There's no escaping it, ever, is there?" I asked quietly. "It will always be with me, this craving for blood."

Ash remained silent as the Mercedes took a corner. "Blood is the constant of a vampire's existence, Candace," he finally said. "No matter what kind of blood we take, it is the one thing we must have to survive. So the answer is no. Being undead can free you from many things, but never from that."

The gates of Ravenswood came into view. I could see a car parked there, heard some sort of commotion.

"That's Bibi," I said, sitting up a little straighter.

"So I see," Ash replied.

He pulled the Mercedes up to the gatehouse, behind Bibi's car. "Good evening, Charlie," he said to the guard as his window slid down. "Is there some sort of problem?"

Before the guard could answer, I heard Bibi's voice. "I want to talk to Candace, Ash," she said. "Right now. I'm not going away until I do, so you might as well get this rent-a-cop to let me in."

I rolled my own window down. "I'm right here, Bibi," I said. "Is everything . . ."

"Not here," Bibi said, cutting me off.

"Charlie, please pass Ms. Schwartz through," Ash said.

"No problem," the security guard replied. "You folks have a good night now."

A moment later, the gates swung open. Bibi drove through first, then pulled over. Ash and I drove past her, and she pulled in behind us. The lights from her car were bright in the rearview mirror.

"Thank you," I said quietly.

"There's no need to thank me," Ash said at once. "Whatever Bibi's feelings for me may be, or mine for her, I know the two of you are close. I only hope her visit here doesn't mean things have gone even worse for Randolph Glass."

"You think Sloane's the one who went after Randolph, don't you?"

"Don't you?" Ash replied, and I heard a sudden bitterness in his voice. "Sloane is ruthless. He'll do anything to get what he wants, but not even I expected him to do this."

"For heaven's sake, Ash," I said. "What happened to Randolph is not your fault."

"No, it isn't," he agreed at once. He took the corner of the street that led to the house. "But that doesn't mean I shouldn't have been more on my guard. The thing is, I can't figure out *why* Sloane went after Randolph. He might have been angry that Randolph won the auction, but there's nothing to gain by the attack as long as the scarab is still at the auction house."

He parked in the drive. By the time I was out of the car, Bibi was already standing on the sidewalk.

"Come inside," I said as Ash unlocked the front door and held it open for us. Bibi walked past him with a defiant toss of her head, but I saw the way she gave a quick, involuntary wince as the front door closed.

The lights in the entry and living room were motion sensitive, keyed to come on low. Ash moved to the panel that controlled the lights, dialed them up another few notches. The stark and lovely living room came into focus.

"I have some business matters to attend to," he said. "And I'm sure the two of you would like to be alone. I'll be in my study if you need me, Candace."

Bibi made a slow circuit of the living room, her high-heeled shoes clicking sharply against the polished wood floor. I saw her pause before a case of Egyptian artifacts. The house was filled with priceless antiquities, objects related to Ash's business.

"This is absolutely stunning," Bibi said at last. "Precisely what I would have expected from Ash. You've done well for yourself, Candace. But then you obviously know that. It's pretty clear you're here by choice."

"Is that why you're here?" I asked. "To insult me? If so, maybe you should go right now." I sighed, realized Bibi was the last person I wanted to fight with, then softened my tone. "We've both had long nights, Bibi. I am genuinely sorry about what happened to Randolph, and about the way I reacted. You called me for support. I let you down. Is Randolph—"

"Recovering," Bibi answered shortly. "They've given him a transfusion. He's stabilized."

"Then why have you come?"

"You can ask me that?" she said. "For the love of God, Candace, you've moved in with Ash. The sonofabitch is a fucking vampire, a fact you seem to have forgotten."

"I haven't forgotten," I said. "And that sonofabitch is the man I love."

"How in hell can you say that?" Bibi exploded. "How can you love him, knowing what he is, what he does?"

"I don't have to explain myself."

"I think you'd damned well better," Bibi all but yelled. "I want to know why the man I love is lying in a hospital with his throat torn out, and you're getting all cozy with a vampire, Candace. I think I deserve that much."

"Bibi," I said holding up my hands. "Ash did not attack Randolph. He wouldn't have. In the first place, the timing isn't right. We've been together since the afternoon. In the second place, it just doesn't make sense."

"Don't be deliberately stupid," she said. "Of course it does. The scarab is missing, Candace. The one from the auction. The one Randolph and Ash both bid on. Randolph made special arrangements to take possession of it early. The last person on the security tapes is the courier from the auction house. Randolph took what Ash wanted, and Ash came to take it back. Randolph fought, so Ash tore his fucking throat out."

"No," I said, moving to her, taking her shoulders between my hands. Bibi was shaking, deep, hard tremors that started in the gut. "That is not what happened, Bibi. Ash wouldn't do that."

"Will you listen to yourself?" she exclaimed, pushing my hands from her shoulders. "You're defending him! You're defending a vampire!"

"Not just any vampire," I said. "We're talking about Ash. I know he did not do this, Bibi. *I know it.*"

The scarab. The scarab is missing, I thought. Now, more than ever, the true culprit seemed plain. It had to be Sloane.

Bibi actually backed away from me then. It would have been a ridiculous, theatrical gesture if it hadn't gone clean through my heart.

"For pity's sake, Candace," she said. "Just how stupid do you think I am? I saw what Randolph looked like before the paramedics arrived. I'm the one who found him. I know what a vampire does to a human body. Don't tell me you've forgotten that, too."

"No," I said. "Of course not."

"Then tell me what the hell you're doing here," she said. "What the hell is going on?"

"I don't think I can answer that," I said. "I'm sorry."

"Then come with me," Bibi said at once. "You simply cannot stay here, Candace. You can't stay with Ash. Surely you can see that much."

"I have to stay with him," I said. "And no, I can't tell you why. Just please believe me when I tell you Ash did not attack Randolph."

"You can't even hear yourself anymore, can you?" Bibi asked. "You sound like an addict coming up with excuses."

I knew that was exactly what I sounded like. And I knew that there was nothing short of the truth that would persuade her otherwise.

"You tell me Ash didn't do this," she went on, her voice furious. "Okay, for the sake of argument, let's say you're right. It doesn't change a goddamned thing. *Ash is a vampire.* Precisely the kind of vampire you once swore you would dedicate your life to stamping out.

"But here you are, singing the same old song. Telling me how much you love him. How in the hell can you do that and still sleep at night? How can you love him knowing what he is, what he does? Your love is going to literally be the death of you, Candace. *You have got to let Ash go.*"

"I can't, Bibi," I said. "I know it seems wrong. But that is the one thing I simply cannot do. It would be better for us both if you stopped asking it of me."

Her face went blank, as if I had struck her so hard a blow, I had wiped all expression from it.

"That's it, then," Bibi said. "We're done. I can't be your friend if you're going to do this, Candace. And *you* shouldn't ask that of *me*. We both know what Ash is capable of. You're not the only one with scars."

She turned toward the door.

"Bibi, don't go like this," I said. "All I'm asking—"

"It doesn't matter, Candace," she said as she spun back around. The emotion was back now. In her voice and in her face. Great silent tears tracked steadily down her cheeks and she made no attempt to stop them.

"You don't have the right to ask anything of me. Not anymore. As of this moment, our friendship is officially over. Somebody else can have the dubious distinction of identifying your body at the morgue."

"Bibi, you don't understand," I said.

"You know what, Candace?" she replied. "You're absolutely right. I have never understood how you can love Ash, knowing what he is. The difference now is that I just don't care anymore."

Once again, she turned to go, hands scrunched deep inside her jacket pockets. And suddenly, Ash was there, materializing as if from thin air. I had no idea if he had heard any of what had passed between Bibi and me. *It doesn't really matter,* I thought.

Bibi started at his sudden reappearance. "You just stay away from me, you undead bastard," she snarled.

As if in slow motion, I watched it happen. Saw the way her right hand rose, straight up, out of her jacket pocket. Her fist was clenched, and in it, something long and straight that caught the light. I was running before I even knew my body was in motion. Stepping between the woman I had trusted more than any other human in the world and the man I loved. As finally, finally, Ash himself began to move, pivoting away from her, turning his body aside. He pulled me with him, and the silver stake Bibi clenched so tightly in her upraised fist missed him and sliced cleanly down my arm. The cut was shallow, not deep enough to kill, the pain more intense than any I had ever known.

I gave a shrill and startled cry, cradling my wounded arm against my body. I felt Ash's arms come up to protect me as he completed the pivot, placing himself between me and Bibi, my face against the wall as he shielded me with his own body. But even as he turned, I heard Bibi's horrified exclamation, the clatter of the silver as it tumbled to the floor.

"*No,*" I heard her gasp. "*Sweet God in heaven, no. No. No!*"

And I knew, in that moment, that our friendship was truly over. Because, in that moment, Bibi knew the truth. My reaction to the silver had given me away. I had not reacted like a human being, but like a vampire.

"Are you all right?" I heard Ash say. "*Answer me, Candace. Are you all right?*"

I swallowed once, then a second time before I could force words up and out of my throat. My arm was throbbing as if Bibi had dragged a red-hot poker down it. "Yes," I said, then swallowed once again. "Ash, I'm fine."

"The hell you are."

I felt his arms fall away then heard Bibi's startled, terrified cry. And then there was a third and final sound: the sound of Bibi's body as it smacked up against the opposite wall. After that, a silence so profound it seemed to me that it had swallowed the entire world. Slowly, leaning against the wall for support, I turned toward that silence.

Bibi was pinned against the wall, trembling and gasping. Her hands were above her head, wrists captured tightly between one of Ash's hands. With his other, he had forced her head back to expose her throat. I watched as he put his mouth upon it, parting his lips so that his teeth rested against Bibi's bare skin.

"Ash," I said, my voice no more than a promise of sound. "No. Don't."

"You are going to listen to me, Bibi," he said, and I knew she felt every single motion of his lips, his teeth against her throat. "And you are going to do exactly what I tell you. . . . You are going to leave this house and never come back. You are going to leave Candace alone. If you hurt her again, in any way, I will do something much, much worse than end your life. I will make you a drone to the end of your days. *My* drone. You will never have an instant of existence that does not have me in it, and I will do my best to make it a living hell. Tell me that you understand me. Nod your head."

Her eyes shut tight now, Bibi managed one shaky nod. Ash stepped back, releasing her as if she were filthy and he could no longer bear to touch her.

"Then we're finished here," he said. "Get out."

She doubled over, clutching her stomach as if in pain—or to prevent herself from throwing up. She staggered down the length of the hallway, crashed against the door. Sobbing openly now, she wrenched it open then dashed out into the night.

Ash turned to me, took me in his arms. "She hurt you," he raged, and I could hear the open anguish in his voice. "She hurt you. I didn't stop it."

"She didn't mean to," I said as I felt my own arms come around him. The burning in my right arm was a little less now. I knew why. The skin near where the silver had touched was dead. "She meant to hurt you."

"And so she did," Ash said. "Just not the way she wanted. You should go to the pool, Candace. The water will help."

"Come with me," I said.

He stepped away, released me then. "No. There is something else that I must do."

Even as I asked, I knew what it was.

"Not a human being, Ash," I said, moving so that I was between him and the open front door. "Promise me it will not be human."

"I can't do that, and you know it. Now get out of my way."

"Ash," I said, my voice breaking even on that single syllable. "For the love of God."

I saw it happen in that moment. Saw the beast inside the man, saw the desperate needs of the vampire. Ash's eyes glowed with a fierce and feral light. His cheekbones stood out in stark relief, as if the skin was stretched over them too tightly. His hands flexed at his sides. His body seemed to ripple, as if struggling to contain that great need inside his own skin.

"Candace," he said, and I heard the almost unimaginable control in his voice, a control he possessed only through the power of his love. "You can't stop this and neither can I. If you love me, if you ever loved me, get out of my way. Right now."

I moved then, no more than a single step, and Ash moved past me, into the night.

I waited up for him, unable to sleep. All that night my thoughts circled: Sloane's attack on me. Whatever it was he wanted with Ash. The scarab. Sloane's attack on Randolph. My house being ransacked. The Board. They were all pieces of a whole, I was sure of it. I just couldn't quite see how those pieces fit together.

Ash came back to me shortly before dawn. I did not hear the front door open, but suddenly I knew he was there. I don't know that I can truly explain how. In the primal fashion that every animal recognizes the nearness of its mate, I suppose. One moment I knew I was alone; the next, I was absolutely certain I was not. I swung stiff legs over the side of the couch and stood. Ash was standing just beyond the reach of the light.

He smelled of blood.

"Candace," he said, and I almost did not recognize the sound of his voice. Weakness and strength, elation and self-loathing. All these were there, all so inextricably bound together they would never be wrested apart. Bibi looked at Ash and saw only evil. I saw so much more.

His voice was quiet when he spoke. "You shouldn't be here. I don't want you here now. Go away. Leave me alone."

I took two steps and watched the way he shifted back.

"No," I said. One single syllable, without heat. "I am not ever going to leave you, Ash. There's no point in asking me to step back. There's no place I can, or want, to go."

"Candace," he said again, a shuddering, tortured gasp of sound. I moved to him then, and this time he did not step away. Bloody as he was, I took him into my arms. He bent his head and buried it against the crook of my neck. "Alive," he choked out. "I left— I didn't—"

I kissed him then and felt the way his body trembled at my touch. "That is part of why I love you," I said. "Now come with me and take your own advice. Let the water soothe you, Ash. Let me soothe you. Let me wash away the blood."

Silently, arms around each other's waists, we walked through the darkened house. When we reached the pool, I eased Ash down onto a seat, knelt to slip off his shoes, then stood and slid out of my robe. I led him into the water fully clothed, glad the water that enveloped us was dark. I did not want to see the way the blood leached away from his clothes, from his body. I dunked his head, and heard him give a gasp of what might be the beginnings of a laugh. Then I stripped the clothing from his body and let it sink to the bottom.

I felt him reach for me then, pulling me to him so that we stood toe-to-toe, pressing me tight along the length of his body. His hands splayed against my back as if he wanted to touch as much of me as possible.

"Feel me, Candace," I heard him whisper against my hair. "Do you feel the way we fit together? There is no part of me that does not love you."

"That makes us even, then," I said. "In spite of the fact that you're taller."

He laughed then, the sound ringing out into the moist darkness. "I can't decide if I am cursed or charmed."

"You are both," I said. "And so am I. It's part of what holds us together, Ash." I slid my hands down his back to cup his ass, felt the way his cock came to life against my thigh.

I reached up, and brought his mouth to mine. There, in the darkness, we made a slow and healing love. The water around us moving as we moved, stroking as we stroked, buoying us up, offering the chance to be reborn. And when it was over, as I held Ash in my arms, I was glad of the water, for it meant he could not know that there were tears upon my cheeks. Even as Ash had filled me, as I had cried out his name in the fierce joy of climax, listened to him cry out mine, I knew the truth.

This could not go on.

He had taken human blood tonight, living human blood. For me. For both of us. But soon, very soon, not even this would be enough. *Which are you, Candace?* I asked myself, as I held Ash tight. *Which will you be?*

Dead or undead. No life at all or vampire. I must make the choice, or I would lose us both.

Twelve

"Tell me about Sloane."

We were in the kitchen, the shades drawn against the bright mid-morning sun. The scent of coffee filled the air. I sat at the counter that ringed the perimeter, perched on a high stool. Ash stood just opposite. The remains of croissants littered two plates. It looked like a normal, human morning, a scene we had deliberately conjured up. As if determined to make everything look as normal as possible while we discussed the far-from-it.

Ash gave me a weary look. "Candace, I've already told you I won't discuss this. For your own safety and—"

"No," I said. "That doesn't work anymore. Sloane not only attacked me, and is apparently after you, but Randolph Glass is now lying in a hospital, half dead. How many more people is Sloane going to take apart before you decide to tell me what you know?"

"I don't know all that much about him," Ash admitted. "I first encountered him in San Francisco, the same night I met you, in fact." He paused for a moment, took a sip of coffee.

You're stalling, Ash, I thought.

"How?"

He glanced up as he set the mug back down on the counter. "What?"

"How did you meet him?" I asked. "Vampire social club?"

"Not precisely," Ash said with an attempt at a smile. "We met because we were . . . selected, I guess you could say. To be competitors in a high-stakes contest."

He paused again and I knew the instant he gave up his internal struggle, just as I knew the reason for it: There was nowhere else to go.

"What sort of contest?" I asked.

"To fill a vacant seat on the Board."

And there it was. Almost literally the last thing Ash and I had quarreled about in a night filled with bitter pain and recriminations. A night that had occurred almost three months ago. A quarrel that had resulted in an utter break between us, an estrangement that had ended only because of Sloane's attack on me. The Board. I had asked about it then, and again after the auction, but Ash had refused to explain, claiming that it was safer for me not to know.

"Who won?"

"Depends on your perspective," Ash said. "Certainly most vampires would say it was Sloane. He is now a member of the Board, able to draw upon their powers, which are considerable. On the downside, in my book anyway, he's also their pawn. To join the Board means absolute dedication to its goals, even at the expense of your own. The only option is absolute obedience to the Board's will. It's either that or be destroyed."

I took a sip of my coffee. "How did he beat you?" I asked. "I would have said, having seen the two of you together, that you're both stronger and smarter than Sloane. He's certainly vicious, but it seems to me that you have more . . . depth."

"Thank you, I think," Ash said, his tone dry. "In the end, it came down to just one thing: Sloane wanted that seat on the Board enough to be willing to pay any price. I was not. The second I stopped playing by their rules, I lost and Sloane won."

I felt something move through me then. Something I wasn't sure I was quite ready to look in the eye.

"What did you do?" I asked.

Ash toyed with the handle on his coffee mug.

"What I *didn't* do turned out to be more to the point," he finally replied. "I did not make you a vampire, nor did I end your life. Your death or . . . conversion, that was my final test before the Board. I failed because I left you alive."

"Why?" I whispered. *"Why?"*

"Because I love you," Ash said simply. "In that elevator, the moment you pulled away, I came to realize just how much."

I put my head down into my hands as the full impact of what he was saying hit home. How many times had I wondered why Ash had left me alive that night? Why hadn't he simply followed me out into the hall and finished me off? And now he was saying the answer was simple: Love.

Suddenly I remembered so many other things about that night. Remembered how very much I had wanted Ash, wanted what he was offering, all of it. I had been a willing participant, right up until the moment I had pulled away.

I could not, in the end, give up my human life, not even for an endless existence with Ash. And I remembered the way he had always claimed that I was not the only one who had paid a price for the events of that night. I had an inkling now of what it had cost.

"What did they do to you?" I asked.

"Nothing," Ash said shortly. "Though not for lack of trying. Fail the test and be destroyed. As far as the Board was concerned, the outcome should have been perfectly straightforward. Unfortunately for them, I had other plans. I left San Francisco that very night, went to ground for an entire year. And I . . . I stayed away from you as long as I could, Candace. I couldn't stay away forever. I'm sorry."

"Don't be," I said. "I'm not."

"I hope to God you mean that," Ash said.

I reached across the counter then, took his hands in mine. "I mean it," I said. "Now let's stop talking about the past. There's nothing to be done about it at this point. Let's talk about the future. What is the Board? What do they want? And what do we have to do to stop them?"

"The Board has existed since the days of the last great Egyptian empire," Ash explained. "Its original members were men, priests of the god Thoth, and it is through him that they still derive their power. Thoth gave mankind speech. It was believed that, through speaking his own name aloud, he had actually created himself.

"But of greatest interest to his priests was the fact that Thoth was a powerful magician who recorded his spells in a volume called *The Book of Thoth*. Among them was a ritual that granted immortality."

"I think I can see where this is going. They tried to perform the ritual, didn't they?"

"They did," Ash nodded. "Unfortunately, they overlooked one thing: *The Book of Thoth* came with a warning. Essentially, the magic it contained was for the use of the gods alone. When the priests invoked the spell, the god Thoth heard their transgression and placed a curse upon their tongues. Instead of becoming immortal, they became undead."

"Vampires," I said. "You're saying they became the first vampires?"

Again, Ash nodded. "In his anger, Thoth removed his book of spells from the world and broke apart his power. He invested it in three tokens, the Emblems of Thoth. He scattered them to the winds and abandoned his perverted followers. But they did not give up. They banded together to form what is now called the Board."

"But surely none of the original members are left," I exclaimed.

"Only one. The leader, who calls himself the Chairman. He is—was—the original high priest of Thoth. He has spent more lifetimes than most people can imagine searching for the Emblems of Thoth, absolutely determined to reunite them, to complete the spell that will make him truly immortal. Invincible. All-powerful. If he succeeds, it means that the Chairman and his followers could never be destroyed. It means they will be gods.

"All the Board members are dangerous, but the Chairman is the most dangerous of all. He has maintained his existence for thousands of years, and every year he has amassed knowledge of some new magic, made himself stronger.

"Drawing power from his followers is part of how the Chairman has survived. The trouble is that, sooner or later, the energy exchange literally burns the lesser vampires out. That is why, throughout its long history, there have been . . . empty seats on the Board. The Chairman uses his followers until they are no longer of any use. Then he replaces them through the sort of contest in which Sloane and I took part."

"But why would other vampires agree to that in the first place?"

"It's not a question of true agreement," Ash replied. "Once they've tagged you—they literally grabbed me off the street—you're in the game, whether you like it or not. Fail, or even fail to try, and you will be destroyed. It is in your best interests to try and win.

"And if you're successful, the power can flow both ways. The Chairman doesn't simply draw power, he invests it also. Individual Board members can make use of the collective power of the Board. And there is always the chance that the Emblems of Thoth will be discovered and reunited while you are a member. Then you, too, will become immortal."

"So if we want to stop them, we have to get to these Emblems first, or at least some of them."

"Some would be the best we can do at this point," Ash replied. "When I went before them, they already possessed one Emblem called the Body of Thoth. Two more remain: the Heart of Thoth and the Tongue of Thoth."

"Wait a minute," I said. "Did you say the *Heart*? Is the Heart the scarab from the auction?"

"I believe so. And I believe that is why Randolph Glass was attacked. They were looking for the scarab, but of course the scarab was still in the safe at the auction house."

"No, that's not true. The heart scarab is gone."

"Are you sure?" Ash's skin had suddenly gone even paler than his normal shade of alabaster.

"When Bibi was here last night, she told me that Randolph made special arrangements to take possession of the scarab early, and that it was stolen from his penthouse when he was attacked."

"Why didn't you tell me this before?"

"I think it's fair to say we had other things on our minds."

"Jesus," Ash said. "This means there's a very good chance that the second of the Emblems is now in the Board's hands. That just leaves one that they don't have: the Tongue of Thoth."

"Any idea where it is?" I asked.

"I don't even know *what* it is," Ash replied. He stepped away from the counter, began to pace the confines of the kitchen, as if thinking aloud. "The first two Emblems are physical objects. The Heart is the scarab. The Body is a pectoral adornment in the shape of Thoth's traditional headdress, a full moon rising from a crescent. From my personal research, I believe the Tongue may be a scroll or some kind of writing. But that's as much as I could unearth. And even that is pure speculation."

"There are hieroglyphics on the back of the picture you gave me," I said. "I've always wondered what they mean."

Ash stopped cold. Slowly, he pivoted on one heel to face me. "What did you just say?"

I flushed. "The picture you gave me in San Francisco, the charcoal sketch you had done in the park. It has an image of Thoth on the back, and there's some kind of writing directly below it."

"You still have that sketch?" Ash asked.

"Well, obviously," I acknowledged, my tone

slightly testy. Given everything that had happened between us since, it was silly to feel so exposed.

"At first I simply forgot about it, to tell you the truth, but when I came home from the hospital in San Francisco, there it was. My first impulse was to tear it up into little, tiny pieces. I went with my second impulse, which was to keep it right where it was."

"On your desk," Ash said slowly, as if even now, more than two years later, he could still envision the details of my small San Francisco apartment.

"That's right. I used it as a daily reminder of all the mistakes I had made, all the places I didn't want to go again. I brought it with me when I moved here. Then, about a year ago, I accidentally broke the glass in the frame. When I took the sketch out of the frame, I discovered the image on the back. I did a little research, and discovered it was Thoth.

"That's how I recognized the mark on Senator Hamlyn's chest," I explained, referring to the politician Ash's vampire soldiers had shot and killed on New Year's Eve—an act I now understood occurred because Hamlyn was under the control of the Board. "It was the same image as the one on the back of the sketch.

"How did you get that paper in the first place?" I asked. "Did you steal it from the Board?"

"No," Ash answered with a shake of his head. "In fact, the original thief was Sloane. Not long after he took it, he came to see me, got a little careless, and I acquired it. I had my picture sketched on the reverse side to cover my tracks."

"And then you gave it to me," I said. "Thanks very much."

"I didn't know what it was at the time, Candace," Ash said mildly. "The truth is, I still don't. But given everything else that's happened, I think we have to assume that this piece of paper is important, if only to Sloane. First he steals the heart scarab from Randolph, then he breaks into your house."

"You think that's why my house was ransacked? To steal back the thing he already stole. But how could Sloane even know I had it?"

"He probably didn't. But even if he found nothing, he knew attacking you, then violating your home, would draw me out. Make us do something foolish."

Ash shook his head, a note of bleak despair edged his voice. "If it is the Tongue of Thoth, then the Board now has all three Emblems."

"No," I said. "They don't."

Before he could question me further, I got down from the stool and hurried to the bedroom. There, on a chair by the bed, was my shoulder bag. I snatched it up then returned to Ash.

"When I left here the day before the auction, I went back to my house," I said. "There was some business I had to take care of, things I wanted kept safe. I saw the sketch, put it in my bag, then forgot I had it."

I pulled it out, set it on the counter, with the image of Thoth facing up. "They don't have it," I said. "We do."

Ash was silent, staring down at the tiny red image of Thoth. So small, it was difficult to make out what it truly was without a magnifying glass. The first time I had seen it, I thought it was a drop of blood.

"Do you know what this means?" Ash said at once. "It means we have leverage. Even if this isn't the Tongue of Thoth, we have a bargaining tool. We can draw Sloane out into the open."

It took about another hour's worth of discussion for us to put a plan in place, examining it carefully from all sides. Our best shot was for me to seek out Sloane. Ash couldn't go because there was a good chance that Sloane, drawing on the powers of the Board, would kill Ash then and there. With me, he might consider a bargain. The risks were enormous, especially to me. If Sloane simply decided to try and finish the job he had already started without asking questions . . .

"We can't afford to worry about that," I insisted to Ash, with more confidence than I actually felt. The thought of being alone with Sloane again was absolutely terrifying. It was also absolutely necessary if we were going to try to take out Sloane and get the scarab back.

"Do you think he'll have the scarab on him?"

"Probably," Ash replied. "He's already lost one item belonging to the Board. The fact that the Chairman may not know this is beside the point. Sloane won't want to run the risk of losing a second. That means he'll keep it as close as possible."

"We're set then," I replied. "All we have to do is put the word out and hope he takes the bait."

"Candace," Ash said slowly, "I want you to promise me something. If anything goes wrong . . ."

"Nothing's going to go wrong," I said quickly.

"Of course not," Ash said. "But if it does, if something happens . . . if the Board catches up with me, if I am taken, I want you to promise that you won't come after me. Don't try to save me. Let me go."

"I can't do that," I answered steadily, though I felt the chill of his words all the way to the bone.

"You wouldn't let me go, so why should I do less for you?"

"Because you are less, Candace," Ash said softly. I made a quick, involuntary movement, and he reached to hold me by the shoulders. "I don't say this to hurt you. I say it because it's the absolute truth, and we both know it. If I am taken, there's a good chance they will destroy me. It's certain they would destroy you. No matter how strong your love, your body is not strong enough to stop them.

"You are the best part of me, Candace, and I never even saw you coming. I want to know that you will still exist, even if I can't be with you."

"But how?" I asked as I felt tears fill my eyes. "How will I exist, Ash? How can I?"

He leaned down, gave me a swift, hard kiss. "That part may be simpler than you know. But before we begin, I'll have your word or we don't do this at all."

"You think we're going to fail, don't you?" I asked. "That's what you're not telling me."

"I don't think that, in fact," Ash said. "I think we have Sloane right where we want him. We have what he wants more than anything else, the scroll. We have the advantage, but there will still be risks. That's why I'm trying to minimize them. I want you to be safe, Candace. As safe as I can make you."

He moved his hands so that they cradled my face. "Promise me. Two words. That's all I ask."

I reached up, took his face in my own hands, brought his lips to mine. Recognized the taste of my own tears even as my mouth moved in consent.

"I promise," I murmured against Ash's mouth.

Thirteen

The vampire community in Vegas is much like the human one, when you get right down to it. Never static, always in flux. But there's one thing that hasn't changed during the time I've lived here. If you want to pass a message through the vampire underground, the Majestic is still the place to go.

The Majestic is in the old part of the Strip, where the original hotels and casinos once stood. Originally an old movie theater, part of its current appeal is its retro decor. Red curtains and gold paint for miles. The Majestic is the biggest and showiest of the fringe places, places where both vamps and humans go. That happens a lot in Vegas, of course, without the human community's knowledge.

I waited until well after midnight when I was sure the joint would be hopping. I dressed in a tight red dress that I sometimes wear when Bibi and I go clubbing. Not exactly subtle when it came to sartorial choices. But then subtle was likely to be lost on Sloane.

I took my own car. I didn't want there to be even the slightest possibility that Sloane could spot Ash and me together, figure out that the whole meeting I was about to ask for was actually a setup. If he thought I was disposable, that's precisely what he'd do. Dispose of me.

I parked several blocks away on a street that at any other time I would have said was too dark for comfort. Tonight, dark was good. Besides, the walk to the club would help me steady my suddenly shaky nerves. *Nerves of Steele,* I reminded myself. But the person who had given me the nickname, the life he had once been a part of, seemed very far away now. Slowly but surely, whether I had fully committed to it or not, I was being drawn deeper and deeper into my existence as a vampire.

I reached the Majestic, pulled open one of the elaborately carved and gilded doors. Originally, the decorations had been frolicking cherubs. When the Majestic became a vampire club, the new owners had turned the cherubs into fat and frolicking baby vampires.

A male vampire with a sculpted body was sitting in the old ticket-taker's cage. "Well hello, gorgeous," he said, his voice as appreciative as his words.

I flashed him a smile. *Could other vampires tell that I wasn't a full-fledged vamp?* I suddenly wondered. Vampires definitely recognize their own kind, even different levels of power among them. Did I read as some low-level wannabe trying to work my way up the ladder? Or would it be something stronger, since the blood that sustained me was that of a powerful vampire?

"Hello yourself," I said. I leaned against the counter on the outside of the cage, giving him a good glimpse of cleavage. "What's the cover?"

The vampire's smile got a little wider. The red dress was a good choice, after all.

"For you, nothing. This time. Maybe next time you'll remember I did you a favor."

Assuming there was a next time, I thought. Still, I had to consider this a positive start to the evening.

"Depends on the favor."

"Nothing out of proportion." The vampire narrowed his eyes, and it came to me suddenly that he was, in fact, having trouble reading me. In which case, I would most likely read as a low-level errand girl for a major big gun. The vampire's next words seemed to validate my hunch.

"Maybe you'll just pass along the fact that I did right by you, that's all," he said. "Good lookin' lady like you, got to be connected."

He's fishing, I thought.

"That sounds fair enough," I said. "Meanwhile, I'm putting the word out that I'm looking to meet someone."

"And who might that be?" the vampire asked.

"Sloane," I said, and watched his eyebrows shoot up. "You know him?"

"*Know* is a bit personal," the vampire replied. The words were offhand, but I could tell he was choosing them with care. "Anyone who's smart knows *about* Sloane. Don't worry, I'm not about to ask why you want him. I know when to mind my own business."

Something else he was no doubt hoping I would pass along.

"So you'll help me get the word out?" I said.

He nodded. "You go on inside. Have a good time."

I moved toward the doors that would take me into the interior of the club, the words the vampire hadn't spoken ringing in my ears.

While you still can. My good-time opportunities were likely to run out if I got on the wrong side of Sloane.

The interior of the Majestic was a seething cauldron of bodies and pounding sounds. Disco music blared from 360-degree speakers. An immense, revolving mirrored ball cast reflections in every direction, and two DJs were spinning discs in perfect sync.

The best thing about the Majestic is that the bar

rings the entire dance floor, which means that, even when the place is packed, you can almost always find a spot. I chose one with a view of the door and ordered my standard mineral water and lime. I wriggled my butt up onto a tall stool, crossed my legs, and kept my eyes open.

So far, so good. I was in. I had put the word out for Sloane. Now all I had to do was sit tight and hope the chance to get at Ash via me was an offer Sloane couldn't refuse.

"*Candace?*" I suddenly heard a voice inquire. I turned to discover that Blanchard Gray had materialized at my side. Until several months ago, Blanchard had functioned as my eyes and ears in the vampire underground. The events of New Year's Eve, the threat of a major showdown between rival vampire factions, had caused him to leave town. I hadn't seen him since, hadn't even known he was back in Vegas.

"Hello, Blanchard," I said. "It's nice to see you. You're looking well."

Blanchard's eyes widened as he took in my attire. Under the lights in the club his bleached-blond hair seemed to almost glow. Blanchard and I share an unusual bond. We met the night a vampire attacked him. I killed the vampire feeding on him then offered him my own blood, allowing him to become one of the undead. It was either that or watch him die in agony.

"It really *is* you," he said, sliding up onto the empty stool beside me. "I wasn't sure at first. You're . . ." He cocked his head. "Different somehow. Though it could just be that dress, of course. Hardly your usual style. So what brings you to the Majestic?"

"The usual reason," I said. "I'm looking for someone. This is the place to come if you want to get the word out. You taught me that, yourself."

"And you paid attention. That is so sweet," he said. He flashed the bartender a devastating smile.

"Please tell me you're not going to order a Bloody Mary," I said.

He gave a shudder. "Perish the thought," he said. And ordered a Lemon Drop. "So, who are you looking for?" he asked as the bartender moved off.

"New guy in town," I said shortly. *And I sincerely hope you don't know him.* "His name is Sloane."

Blanchard hissed out an alarmed sound through his perfect white teeth. "Candace, angel, far be it from me to tell you your business, but have you by any chance gone completely nuts? I've been back in town all of three days and even I know to steer clear of that one."

"I'm just doing what I have to, Blanchard," I said. "You know how that goes."

The waiter brought his drink then, sparing him the need to reply. He took a sip, his eyes on the dance floor.

"Can I ask you something, Blanchard?" I suddenly said.

"About anything but my love life," he replied. "Not that I wouldn't be happy to discuss it, if I weren't going through a dry spell, you understand."

"You are so full of crap," I said.

He smiled. "I know. What's the question?"

"Do you hate me?" I asked. "For what happened that night?"

"Why should I hate you?" Blanchard asked at once. I could tell the question had surprised him. It surprised me, too. I hadn't realized how much I wanted to ask it until the words were actually coming out of my mouth.

"You weren't the one who took away my life," Blanchard went on. "Without you, I would have no existence at all. What I have may not be perfect, but it's a damn sight better than nothing."

"And you really mean that?" I said.

"Of course I do," Blanchard answered. "Candace, what is this about? Are you afraid Sloane's going to put the bite on you? If so, why the hell are you waiting around?"

"Actually," I said, "it's a little more complicated than that. Believe me when I say you don't want to know. You might not even want to be seen with me, in fact."

"Oh, great!" Blanchard exclaimed. "*Now* you tell me."

"Candace Steele." A voice I recognized all too well slid through the sound pulsing through the bar. "What a lovely surprise. And looking so lovely, too. I'm surprised Ash let you out of his sight."

And there he was, standing on the edge of the dance floor like a slice of night. If I didn't know what a cold-blooded killer he was, Sloane would have looked dangerous and romantic, his dark clothing only serving to highlight his pale skin, dark hair and eyes. The scar I had given him ran like a fault line down the right side of his face.

To me, he just looked dangerous. Dangerous as hell.

I took a sip of mineral water. It's difficult to bandy words when your throat is dry as dust.

"Ash doesn't run me," I replied. "He just thinks he does."

"Don't tell me. And you let him go right on thinking that," Sloane answered, his tone delighted. "This just gets better by the minute, doesn't it?"

His eyes cut to Blanchard, who was watching the exchange between us with the same sort of fascination a deer gives to oncoming headlights.

"You snuck away from Ash to meet some Nancy boy?"

"I snuck away from Ash to meet you," I said. "Nancy just happens to be taking up adjacent space." Best for all concerned if Sloane thought Blanchard and I didn't know one another. He grinned then, and Blanchard blinked as if snapping out of a trance.

"Not for very much longer," Sloane said.

Without a word, Blanchard slid off the stool and disappeared into the crowd on the dance floor, leaving his unfinished drink behind on the bar. Sloane took his place on the stool, his eyes on the dancers.

"I hear you want to see me."

"You hear right."

"Flattered as I am, I can't imagine what for."

"Simple," I said. "Ash wants to arrange a meet, but he thought you might . . . misunderstand if he came himself. He sent me as his emissary."

"Oh, really. Why the hell should I want to meet with Ash?" Sloane inquired. "Why shouldn't I just hunt him down and destroy him?"

"You think the two are mutually exclusive?"

Sloane's head turned toward me as if pulled by a string. I definitely had his full attention now.

"So he's told you," he said. "I wondered if he had."

I managed a laugh though my stomach had abruptly knotted up, tight.

Sloane cocked his head, his dark eyes holding mine. I could tell he was trying to figure all the angles. He slid his hand across the bar top to run his fingers down my bare arm. I felt myself jolt.

"You know," he said quietly, and I heard both syllables, every nuance within them, even over the noise of the club. "I always wondered how Ash could give up so much just for a woman. I think I'm beginning to see the point."

"You know what they say about flattery, don't you?" I replied.

Sloane laughed then, sliding off the stool, pulling me with him. "Come dance with me, Candace," he said. "I suddenly discover I have the need to feel you in my arms."

Every instinct in my body was screaming like a wild thing, telling me to pull back, pull away. Every cell of my body conscious of the excruciating pain that had come the last time Sloane held me in his arms. I clamped down, hard, with my mind. Forced myself to stand still. I was not ruled by instinct. Not entirely, not just yet.

"I came to talk," I said. "Not to socialize."

"You think the two are mutually exclusive?" Sloane inquired, parroting my words with a wicked smile. "You could put up a fight, of course. That might be fun, too."

"You are such an obvious bastard," I said.

Sloane smiled sweetly. "I'm so glad you noticed."

He pulled me out onto the dance floor.

Dancing with Sloane was sort of like undergoing torture. You can see trouble coming straight at you, and there's nothing you can do to avoid it. Not only that, you have no idea how long it's going to go on. Even as I felt his arms slide around me to bring me in close, I told myself that I could take it. I wasn't the quarry Sloane wanted. This was just his way of showing who was in control.

He held me right up against him, full-body contact. One hand wrapped tight around my rib cage, pressing my breasts against his chest. The other wandered, working its way slowly but surely toward my ass, as if he actually believed I might find that exciting. For one split second, I considered playing along, then abandoned the idea. That good an actress I'm not. Sloane's touch filled me with nothing but loathing, and he knew it. He bent his head, his lips at the base of my throat, then trailing up the side of my neck to tease my ear.

"I remember how you taste, Candace," he murmured. "Very, very sweet."

I turned my head, pressed my own lips to the scar that marred the right side of his otherwise perfect face.

"You aren't the only one who remembers things, Sloane."

I felt his body stiffen, knew I had won a battle, though hardly the whole war. His hands stopped moving, and his hold loosened, ever so slightly.

"So what the hell does Mr. Ashford Donahue the third think he has to offer me that I can't just come and take myself?"

"The possibility of a partnership, for one thing," I replied. "A genuine one, rather than the somewhat lopsided arrangement you're involved in now. He said you once suggested such a course of action in San Francisco. All he's looking to do is to follow up."

Sloane gave a short laugh. "Oh, is that all," he mocked. "Ash never does anything halfway, Candace. You of all people ought to know that." He leaned back then, studying my face once more. "Then again, maybe you don't."

Don't let him play you. Don't get sidetracked, I chanted to myself.

"You do a nice imitation of the pot calling the kettle black," I replied, knowing it was time to play my final card. "I'm under the impression that you lost something in San Francisco during a meeting with Ash. An item he still has in his possession. A fact your masters may not be aware of. Ash is simply trying to offer you the opportunity to discuss the situation—for old time's sake—before he takes any steps to set the record straight and return the item to its rightful owners.

"I imagine they'll be very grateful to finally know the truth, don't you? But if you're not interested, all you have to do is say so."

I felt his hand seize the back of my hair, pulling my head back in a painful grip, one that exposed my throat.

"You little bitch," he said. "You know where it is, don't you? You're going to tell me. Right now."

"I really don't think you understand," I said, fighting to keep the pain from my voice. "I'm just the messenger and nothing more. You want to talk more, know more, you have to see Ash, up close and personal. He picks the place and time. Those are odds you ought to be able to understand, Sloane. They're the same ones you yourself would offer."

He released me with a suddenness that left my head flopping on my shoulders.

"You think you're so smart, both of you. Tell me something, Candace, do you like your new existence? I have to say it wouldn't appeal much to me, being neither one thing nor the other. But that's where Ash is clever, isn't he? Giving you a taste of the good life, letting you experience firsthand what it has to offer. He's betting there'll be no way you'll want to return to being human after that. Particularly since the only way to accomplish it would be to kill him."

"I don't know what you mean," I said, the words out before I could stop them.

"It's really very simple," Sloane replied, and I could hear the satisfaction in his voice. "So simple, Ash really should have mentioned it long before now. You want to be human again, truly human? Then take Ash out. If he doesn't exist as a vampire, neither do your ties to him. You'll go back to being a living, breathing human being."

I felt the shock of Sloane's words ripple through my body. *No, it isn't true. It can't be true,* I thought. I didn't speak aloud, but my reaction was impossible to miss, or to misunderstand.

"I know just how you feel." Sloane's voice was suddenly murmuring in my ear. "It's so terrible to be betrayed by the one you trust the most. But that's the beauty of the present situation, Candace. Don't you see? You have the chance to turn the tables now. You can betray Ash and he'll never see it coming."

"I can't think. I need to think," I gasped, pulling backward. "Just let me go to the ladies' room," I said. Oldest trick in the book. When in doubt, head for the loo.

I took several stumbling steps away. Sloane stayed right with me. When we reached the edge of the dance floor, he grasped one arm to hold me back.

"You wouldn't be thinking of trying anything foolish, like sneaking out on me, would you?" he asked.

I jerked my arm away. "Don't be ridiculous," I snapped. "What I want is a few moments of peace so I can decide whether I want you to roast Ash over a slow fire or boil him in oil. And I better have some say in the matter, Sloane."

He gave a full-bodied laugh that told me I had pleased and surprised him. I took a step away, but Sloane reached out once more, jerked me back with enough force to show who was in charge.

"I wouldn't get too accustomed to giving orders."

I leaned my head back, looked him straight in the eye. "I don't intend to become accustomed to anything to do with vampires. You think I'm too stupid to figure out why you shared Ash's dirty little secret? Think again. You want me to hand him over, to help you get back the thing you stole.

"And I just might be willing to do it, on one condition. I get the same ultimate benefit you do: immortality."

Sloane's eyebrows shot sky high. "That's a pretty steep price."

I kept my gaze and my voice steady. "Bet the Chairman wouldn't think so," I replied. "He gets what may be the third Emblem of Thoth and an end to the only vampire to ever successfully defy him. In fact, I think I just became the Board's best and newest asset. But if you don't see it that way, I can always go to the Chairman myself."

"You cocky little bitch," he snarled. "How about I just rip your throat out right here and now?"

"Now who's being stupid?" I replied. "You've just turned me into the perfect weapon, and we both know it. You destroy me now and you walk out the door the same way you came in: one Emblem short. You agree to my deal, I give you the possibility of giving the Chairman what he's spent his entire existence searching for. I imagine he'd be very grateful, don't you?"

I jerked free of his grasp, stepped back.

"Where the hell do you think you're going?" Sloane barked.

"To the ladies' room," I said, opening my eyes wide and innocent. "Assuming I still have your permission."

"Go on, go powder your nose," he said. "But when you come back out, you better be prepared to take me to Ash."

You have no idea just how prepared I'll be, I thought.

Miraculously, the ladies' room was empty. The music from the dance floor was piped in but turned down low. Here, the original opulence of the Majestic's movie house days still held sway. The floor was marble, as was the long makeup counter at the far end of the room. I walked to it, sank down onto one of the velvet-cushioned seats that dotted its length. Then I leaned my arms on the counter and dropped my head down onto them. Grateful, so grateful to be alone.

Sonofabitch, I thought. *Sonofafuckingbitch. Why the hell didn't you tell me, Ash? What have you done?*

All this time he had watched me struggle with the two options before me: drink living blood and become a true vampire, or truly die. And never once had he so much as hinted there was a door number three, a way that I could return to being fully human once more.

Wait a minute, Candace, I thought.

I lifted my head, then gazed at the place in the mirror where my reflection should be. Hadn't Ash begged me not to come after him if he was taken, if something went horribly wrong with our plan to use Sloane to get to the Board? Because he'd known that the end of his existence would set me free. He'd known all along, and he never wanted me to know.

"*Ask anything else you want of me,*" Ash had begged the night of Sloane's attack. "*I will do anything else you want, but do not make me watch you die.*"

And now he had given me the same gift, concealing from me the only way that I might be free, the only way I could return to the world of sun, reclaim the life that I had lost. The price of my ticket back into the human world was steep but simple. It was nothing less than Ash himself.

No! I thought. *I will not pay it. Not now. Not ever.* Such a price was way too high. I had let Ash make me what I was not simply because I was afraid of dying, but because I wanted him, wanted to spend eternity in his arms. Not because of fear, but because of love.

You are clever, Sloane, I thought. *But not quite clever enough.* It would never occur to him that I could come to view Ash's sin of omission not as a sin, a betrayal, but as an act of love, the ultimate sacrifice.

And it's up to me to make sure he doesn't have to make it, I thought. There was just one way to do that: by stopping the Board.

Much as everything in me cried out against putting Ash in danger, we had both come too far to turn back now. Forward was the only option open to us, the only direction left.

Steadier now, I sat up straight, gazing in the mirror at the place where my reflection would have been if I were truly alive. I could no longer see who I had been. I could only feel who I was now. *I am Candace Steele,* I thought, *and I am a vampire.* No doubts, no regrets, no second guesses. If I was going to help defeat the Board, this is how I would do it. Not as a human, but as a vampire. Sloane had actually handed me a stronger weapon to get at him. He would believe his little secret had turned me against Ash because anger and resentment are what Sloane is made of.

I closed my eyes then, reaching for that place deep inside me, the undead zone. Reaching for the unique rapport I shared with Ash, strong because our blood bond was strong. *Come to me, my love,* I thought. *Give me your power. Use my body as your own.*

This was our secret weapon, the thing that Sloane would never think to look for. Ash and I would fight together. Together, we would take back what Sloane had stolen. What would become of us in the future could be decided when the battle with Sloane and the Board was finally over.

Fourteen

Sloane was waiting right where I left him. His eyes lit as I approached.

"Ready?" he asked.

"As I'll ever be," I answered. He slid off the stool, holding me lightly by one arm, and we began to make our way to the door. "You do realize this was supposed to be a double cross."

"Of course." He pulled the door open and we stepped out into the cool evening air. "Though I'm a little surprised Ash went for the obvious choice."

"Maybe he figured it was so obvious, you'd assume he wouldn't choose it," I said. We hit the sidewalk, and I turned left. "I even parked my car in a nice secluded spot."

Sloane slowed our pace by exerting pressure on my arm. "We could always take mine."

"Please don't tell me you came in anything so prosaic as an internal combustion vehicle," I said.

Sloane laughed, low in his throat. *Good, very good,* I thought. Everything about him exuded confidence. But Ash and I were joined now. I could feel his power dancing like electrical current just beneath my skin. Feel his eagerness to take this longtime adversary down. It was sort of like being a walking, talking kaleidoscope. Even just progressing down the street had facets, possibilities to it that I had never noticed before. I looked like Candace Steele, walked and talked like her, but those moments alone had made me something more. I was Ash and Candace now, joined in the ultimate rapport.

"Besides," I went on as Sloane and I crossed the street—only two more blocks to go. "We deviate from the plan in any way and Ash is bound to get suspicious."

"Can't have that, can we?" commented Sloane.

We traversed the second crosswalk then bore right, down a small side street. At once, everything grew darker, more remote. I swallowed, but my throat was bone dry. About another block now. I could feel the way Sloane tensed, almost heard his neck muscles strain with the effort he was making to look only straight ahead. Not to give away the fact that he expected an attack by glancing side to side.

"There is just one thing I should mention," I said.

"And what is that?" Sloane replied.

Quick as lightning, I twisted from his grasp, pivoted, then drove the flat of my hand up, hard, beneath his jaw, feeling Ash's power sing up my arm. Sloane staggered back, blood gushing from his mouth.

"It's still a double cross."

With a howl of rage, Sloane lunged. I danced out of range, cursing my high-heeled shoes.

"You little *bitch*," Sloane gasped out. He ran a hand across his mouth, flicked blood away with his fingers.

"You keep calling me that," I said. "I think we need to work on your vocabulary, Sloane. There are so many more interesting ways to describe a woman. Particularly a strong one."

He lunged for me once more. I felt Ash's power surge inside me. And then, for how long I never quite knew, I lost myself. Somewhere, I was still Candace Steele. I moved with her body, saw with her eyes. But the power, the strength, the hatred of my adversary, all those belonged to Ash. My body might not be as strong as his, but he used it well. Like the smallest child on the playground, the one school bullies love to pick on, until the child learns to use its small size to its advantage and goes on the offensive instead of simply cowering. Darting forward to land quick blows then dancing out of range, refusing to close with Sloane. I could feel his anger and frustration like a third member of the fight.

We're going to do it, Ash. We're going to win, I thought.

Then, literally as if from nowhere, I heard the rev of an engine. Headlights speared into my eyes. With a squeal of brakes, a car lurched to a halt at the curb not ten paces from where I fought with Sloane. I heard doors open and the sound of people getting out. I had no idea who the newcomers were, but I was aware that they left the engine running.

Trapped! I'm trapped, I realized.

If I stepped into the street, I'd be in the path of the car. If I moved toward the closest building, Sloane could pin me, just as he had done before. That left two options. I could turn and run away, or I could run toward Sloane.

In the time it took me to recognize my options, I was moving. Forward, still the only direction there was. Screaming like an Amazonian on the battlefield, I ran straight at Sloane. No more than an arm's reach away, I caught a flash of movement to my right. And suddenly, Ash was there, in person, stepping between us, lunging toward Sloane, grabbing for his throat.

I felt a flash of panic. *Would Ash be strong enough to fight Sloane?* And in that instant of doubt, our rapport broke, and I knew we were each on our own.

Sloane knew it, too. He slammed Ash to the ground, and I heard his body hit pavement with a sickening thud. Without thinking, I launched myself at Sloane, grabbing for his arm. He lunged for me instead, his shoulder ramming into my ribs like a battering ram. With a scream, I went down. I just had time to see Ash get to his feet and spin toward me before strong arms seized me, hauled me to my feet, forced me on unwilling legs toward the car. The back passenger door was open. I kicked out, desperately struggling to throw my captor off-balance and free myself. Instead, I found myself facedown on the seat, a body covering mine.

"Go!" I heard a voice call out. With a jerk that almost hurled me from the seat, the car shot forward. I was flailing wildly now. Striking out at anything within reach, desperate to force a way out, to get back to Ash.

"For God's sake, Candace," the same voice exclaimed. "Stop fighting. You're safe now."

Just as the car rounded the corner, I managed to sit up, hurling myself sideways, pulling up on the door handle with all my might. My shoulder crashed

painfully into the door. Locked, locked tight. I began
to sob then, a wild and frantic sound, twisting my
body to look out the back window. I couldn't see
Ash anymore. But I could see Sloane. One arm
raised, fist clenched, and then the fist came down.
Again. Again. Again. It was still rising and falling
when the car completed the turn and he was lost to
sight.

"Oh, Carl," I gasped. "What have you done?"

The rest of the trip was accomplished in a daze
of horror, a nightmare of total silence. Once I realized there was no more reason to fight, I did my
best to take stock of my surroundings. I was in an
unmarked police car. Chet was driving. I could see
his face in the rearview mirror as we passed beneath the streetlights, saw the way his worried eyes
kept flicking toward the backseat. After about three
minutes, I knew where we were going: Bibi's town
house. I leaned back and closed my eyes. And it
was only then that I realized Carl had his arms
wrapped around me, holding me tight. And I remembered, suddenly, what had happened the last
time Carl had held me in his arms.

I shifted out of them, as far away as I could. "Let
me go, Carl. It's not as if you've left me an escape
route anyhow."

"You're welcome, Steele," Carl said shortly. "We just saved your ass back there, or didn't you notice?"

"You don't know anything about it," I said.

"You're damn right I don't," Carl responded. "But that sure as hell is going to change before the night is over."

Chet pulled the police car up in front of Bibi's condo, popped the locks on the backseat doors, then switched the car off. As soon as he heard the locks click, Carl put a hand on my arm.

"You even think about running and I'll have you in cuffs before you can blink," he said.

"Gee, thanks," I answered. "Good to know."

In silence, the three of us walked the short distance to the entrance to Bibi's town house, Chet on one side, Carl on the other. Carl kept a tight grip on my arm. Chet didn't touch me. *So he knows,* I thought. Had Bibi told him, or had he figured it out for himself? Not that it mattered much. I wondered what they'd said to Carl to get him to participate in the night's events.

Chet rang the bell.

"Hello?" Bibi's voice sounded through the door almost at once.

"Bibi, it's Chet," he said. "We've got her."

Bibi opened the door at once. When she saw me,

she made a strange, jerky movement, as if uncertain whether she wanted to hug me or lash out. Instead she stepped back, holding the door open wide. Chet stepped through first, then me, still attached to Carl.

The second we were all inside, I shook off Carl's arm. "So what is this, some sort of intervention?"

Now that the initial shock of what had happened was wearing off, I could feel the adrenaline begin to course through my body once more. Unable to stand still, I paced Bibi's living room like a caged tiger.

Ash, I have to get back to Ash, I thought.

"You can't keep me here against my will," I said. "You've got no right."

Bibi's face looked pale and strained, but her voice was firm when she finally spoke. "We're your friends, Candace. We're just trying to help."

I stopped pacing, spun around.

"Help?" I all but shouted. "How can you help when you don't know what the hell is going on?"

"Then why don't you tell us?" Carl put in. His voice sounded calm, but I knew him well enough to recognize the sound. This was his interrogate-the-suspect voice.

"No," I said. *Calm down, Candace,* I was chanting in my head. *Calm down.* If I acted too crazy,

Carl could put me in a cell. Then I'd never be able to help Ash.

"I'm sorry, but I can't do that, Carl," I went on. "Please believe me when I say you don't really want to know."

He crossed the room in two quick strides, seized me by both arms. "I'm tired of hearing that you're sorry," he rapped out. "And I think the statute of limitations on 'please believe me' is all used up. I want to know what's going on, Candace, and I want to know now. What kind of trouble has this Donahue gotten you into? Are you going to tell me what this is all about?"

"No," I said again, making my voice as steady as I could. "I'm not. *I can't tell you what's going on, Carl.* I want you to be safe, and the only way you can be is if you don't know. Something my well-intentioned, high-minded friends here might have remembered before they dragged you into this."

"For Christ's sake, Candace," Carl said, giving me a shake. "I'm a cop, not a kid. If Chet and Bibi can handle whatever this is, I sure as hell can."

"That's not the point," I replied. "You ask them. Ask them if knowing helps them feel safer, if it helps them sleep better at night. Then ask them what the hell business they had bringing you along for the ride."

"All right, Candace," Bibi snapped. "I think

you've made your point. Much as I hate to say it, she's right, Carl. I guess you could say I brought you into this situation under false pretenses. I'm sorry, but it's better for you not to know."

"Please," I said, reaching to hold Carl back now. "Just do this for me, Carl. Stop asking questions and go home. What I am involved in is dangerous. I want to know that you are safe, that just one person I have loved in the day-to-day world is untainted and whole. If you ever cared about me at all, walk away, Carl."

Carl's mouth had a funny crook to it, as if he was trying not to laugh or cry. "That's manipulative and you know it," he finally said.

I felt my own mouth twist. "Whatever it takes to get the job done. I don't want to hurt you, Carl. And I don't want to be responsible for getting you hurt."

"Sometimes it happens anyway," he replied.

"I know. So you do the best you can; you play the odds. I want you out of the game now, while there's still time."

He took one of my hands in his, then pressed his lips into the center of my palm. And for a moment I feared I would break down. Scream out my pain and fear for Ash, for Carl, for myself.

"You know where to find me if you need me,"

Carl said as he let me go. "And don't think this means I'm going to let you off the hook forever."

"I know," I said. "I won't. Thank you, Carl."

Without another word, he turned to Bibi. "I'll expect you to stay in touch. And next time you decide you want my help, you can expect me to want some answers up front."

He strode to the door, let himself out.

I counted the seconds, ignoring Bibi and Chet, waiting for the cruiser to pull away.

"Candace," Bibi began.

"I don't have time for this bullshit," I said, then started for the door.

Bibi planted herself solidly in front of it. "You're not going anywhere."

"Get out of my way, Bibi," I said.

"Why?" she challenged. "So you can go back to Ash? Is that who you are now, Candace? Is it what you are? You finally gave in, gave him what he wanted so now it's all about him."

"That isn't how it happened!" I cried. "You're so sure you know everything, when in fact you don't know one single fucking thing about what's going on.

"I was as good as dead, Bibi. If not for Ash, I would *be* dead. He did what he had to do to save me, and yes, for the record, I asked for it. You try staring death straight in the face and see what choice you make."

"I don't believe you," Bibi said, but I could see my revelation had shaken her. "*I don't believe you.* You love him. You've always loved him."

"That's right. I have," I said. "And you know what the big problem with that is? I didn't recognize it in time. You go on believing Ash is the one and only bad guy in the world. Personally, I'm putting my money on Sloane."

"Sloane?" Bibi asked.

"The other bidder for the heart scarab," I said impatiently. "Another vampire. He's the one who attacked Randolph; he attacked me. Ash and I were setting a trap for him tonight. That's what your little rescue interrupted. Now Sloane has Ash, and I have no idea where to find him. I only know I've got to get to him before it's too late. Now you can get out of my way, or I can make you. Either way, I'm going."

"Too late for what, Candace?" Chet's quiet voice asked even as, with a quick jerky movement, Bibi stepped aside.

"Something bad is coming," I said, my hand on the doorknob. "Ash may be our only hope of stopping it."

"What is it?" Chet asked at once. "What's coming?"

Pain surged through me then, utterly without

warning. A hot and brutal sear of lightning straight through my chest. I dropped to my knees with a cry. Through the roaring that filled my ears, I thought I heard Bibi's voice. Desperately, I waved her back.

"Don't touch me," I managed. "Don't."

A second wave took me then. I threw my head back, body trembling with effort as I tried to let the pain roll through me. If I fought it, it would shatter me to pieces. I felt my vision dim. Then, for one instant, it sharpened. Absolutely everything within my field of vision was crystal clear. And what I saw around me wasn't Bibi's living room, but what looked like two great shoulders of red roche, one slightly higher than the other. As if some giant with a crooked back had become immortalized in stone. I had a sense of motion, of being propelled directly toward them. Pain exploded through my head, so bright and hot that I saw stars. Then both it and the vision faded out. I dropped my head. My arms gave way and I fell onto the carpet.

"Candace, for God's sake," Bibi said. I felt her kneeling beside me.

"Okay," I managed. "I'm okay. Just give me a minute."

"I'll go get a glass of water," I heard Chet say. I rolled over onto my back, closed my eyes, listened to his footsteps depart then return.

"Can you sit up?" he inquired.

"I think so," I said. I managed it after a moment. With Bibi's arm around me, I got to my feet, made it to the closest chair. Chet handed me the water and I took a few sips.

"What just happened, Candace?" he asked quietly.

"I think," I answered slowly, "that it was a moment of rapport with Ash. I felt what he felt, saw what he saw. For a few seconds, I wasn't in this room anymore. I was somewhere in the mountains. I—" My voice broke, and I forced myself to go on. "I think they're torturing him."

"Who are they, Candace?" Chet asked steadily. "Tell us what's really going on."

I gave way to my fears and my own pain then. Dropping my face down into my hands, I wept like an abandoned child.

"I've failed him," I said. "He saved me and now I can't help him."

"Then let us help you," Chet said. "You said something bad is coming. Tell us what it is so we can help you fight it."

"I warn you, I'm going to sound insane," I said as I scrubbed at the tears on my cheeks. It would do no good to break down. If Ash was weak, if he was in pain, I had to stay strong, in more ways than one.

"There's a group of vampires called the Board. They're incredibly powerful and completely evil. Sloane is one of them. They're trying to perform an ancient ritual that will make them immortal."

"Immortal?" Bibi said.

"I told you it would sound insane," I reminded her. I began to speak rapidly now, wanting to get it all out. "To complete the ritual the Board needs three objects—they're called the Emblems of Thoth. Two are already in their possession. The first they've had for a long time. But the second is the scarab that Randolph won at that auction. That's why Sloane stole it from him."

I saw a flicker of belief flash through Bibi's eyes. "So it really was Sloane who attacked Randolph?"

I nodded.

"What about the third Emblem?" Chet asked.

"We have it," I said. "Or we think we do, Ash and I. There are hieroglyphics on it. Ash managed to translate some of it but it seemed meaningless. We were running out of time. So we put together a plan to slow the Board down, to try and grab the scarab back from Sloane. That's what your little *rescue* interrupted. Thanks to you, the whole thing got screwed up. Now Sloane has Ash and . . ."

At the thought of the pain I'd felt, what Sloane must have done to Ash to cause it, my voice cracked and I broke off.

"Where is the Emblem now?" Chet asked, after a moment.

"At Ash's house," I said. And suddenly I saw what must be done. "We have to figure out what it really means," I said. "We have to try."

"And if we do, then what?" Bibi asked.

"Then we do whatever it takes to get to Ash and try to stop the Board."

Fifteen

"Well," Bibi said, a short time later, and I could tell she was struggling to find the right tone. "This is all we needed, ancient Egyptian vampires. I'll never be able to set foot in the Luxor again."

We were in Chet's car on the way to Ash's house, to find the piece of paper that might now be our only way to stop the Board. Chet had offered to help translate the hieroglyphics. I was dubious. If Ash couldn't make sense of them, what luck would Chet have? Still, I accepted Chet's offer of help, and the three of us had formed a slightly uneasy alliance.

We sat together now, across Chet's front seat, Bibi hugging the passenger door as if she still wasn't quite sure she really wanted to touch me. I wasn't sure I could blame her, but still, it hurt. *She's Bibi; she's agreed to help you, Candace,* I thought. *That's what counts.*

"There's something I don't understand," Chet

suddenly spoke up as we approached the Ravens-wood gates. After a quick glance into the car, the security guard passed us through. "If this third Emblem is on a piece of paper, why don't you just destroy it? Wouldn't that prevent the ritual from being performed?"

"It would," I admitted. "But it would also leave the Board operational and whole. What Ash wanted, what we both want, is a way to stop the Board, once and for all. He believed that by possessing the Emblems himself, he might be able to use their power against the Board. I don't understand very much of this, but Ash has been studying the Board and its history for years."

"Maybe translating the hieroglyphics will help us understand," Chet said.

"Let's hope so," I replied.

A few moments later, I was ushering Chet and Bibi into the house, trying without success to push my worry for Ash to the back of my mind. But I could still feel it, humming through my veins, making me nervous and jumpy in spite of my weariness.

"The study's at the end of the hall," I said. "I'll go get the paper, then meet you there. Go ahead and power up the laptop. Do whatever you need to get set up."

Quickly, I walked to the bedroom, retrieved Ash's picture from my shoulder bag. I did my best not to focus on the room, itself. Not Ash's shirt, thrown casually over the back of the chair by the bed. Definitely not the bed, itself. If I gave way to my fears, my sense of loss, I would stumble on the path I had laid out for myself.

Who the hell are you kidding, Candace? I thought. I'd fall and be unable to get up. I was all but on my knees now, facing the worst-case scenario. Me, alone, against the Board. *And you'll never get anywhere if you stand around feeling sorry for yourself, now will you?* I thought. *Besides, you're not alone. You have two friends right down the hall. Friends who are putting themselves in danger just by being here.* I pivoted, walked swiftly out the bedroom door, quietly closed the door behind me.

"That's Ash's picture," Bibi said, her tone surprised, when I returned to the study.

"Actually," I said, as I turned it over and placed it on the desk, "Ash's picture is just camouflage. This is the thing that is important." I gestured to the tiny red image visible in the lower-right-hand corner. "The image itself is called the Mark of Thoth. What we need to figure out is what the hieroglyphics underneath it mean."

Chet squinted intently at the hieroglyphics. "It can't hurt for me to try. Sometimes a fresh pair of eyes . . . Maybe Ash was too close to the problem." He lifted up his glasses, made a face, then dropped them back down onto his nose. "Actually, the whole thing is kind of hard to see."

"There's an *OED* on the bookshelf," I said, going over to it and retrieving the magnifying glass.

"Great," Chet replied as I handed it to him. He held the glass over the small red splotch, squinting again. "Okay, okay. This is good. The image itself is very definitely Thoth. He's wearing that crescent headdress and holding a papyrus in one hand."

Bibi gave a sudden shudder. "This Egyptian stuff is starting to creep me out. All those human bodies with animal heads."

Chet nodded again. "It is pretty primal stuff. So, what we have is three basic hieroglyphs . . ." His voice trailed off.

"I'll leave you to it, then," I said, making quick eye contact with Bibi. She nodded. Together, we left the study. I don't think Chet even noticed we were gone.

"I have to take care of a couple of things," I said. "Not to sound weird but, make yourself at home."

"You don't want company?" she asked quickly.

"Maybe a little later," I said.

"Ash has been a vampire for a long time, hasn't he?" she asked suddenly.

"Not compared to the Board. But long enough so that it's hard for me to imagine." I reached out, touched her on the arm. She twitched slightly, as if her mind was overriding her body's natural instinct to pull away. "You sure you'll be all right? You could stay with Chet."

"No," she said, with a shake of her head. "I'll be fine."

I let my hand drop away. "I won't be too long."

"Okay," she said. And it came to me suddenly that I couldn't ever remember hearing Bibi sound so lost.

"Thanks for coming, Bibi."

"Oh, hey," she said. "Fearless vampire-killer, that's me."

"I'm glad to hear that one of us is fearless," I replied.

I turned, then moved off down the hall. The last thing I saw before I turned the corner, out of sight, was Bibi standing with her hand over the place my fingers had touched.

I went to the pool. Stripped down, I entered the cool water, felt it enclose me in its satin depths. *Cleanse me,* I thought. *Heal me. Heal Ash. Help us to be reborn.*

I ducked my head under, propelled myself through the soft, cool dark. I surfaced at the far end of the pool, treading water for a moment then lifting myself up onto the shelf where Ash and I had once made love. I stretched out, resting one hand on my arm while, with my other hand, I trailed my fingers in the water. Doing nothing more complicated than savoring the feel of the liquid against my skin.

I'm sorry, Ash, I thought. *I hope you'll understand.*

I was going to break my promise.

I was going to go after Ash even though my chances of success were so slim as to be almost impossible. If Ash thought I was going to leave him to face the Board alone . . . he didn't know me very well.

"I will never abandon you, Ash," I whispered. "Not while any part of me can still make a choice."

I heard a sound then, at the end of the pool. I lifted up my head. "Bibi, is that you?" I called.

"Oh, Candace," she said, and I could tell by her tone that she was embarrassed. "I'm sorry. I didn't mean to disturb you. I just thought . . . if the pain should come back. I know you wanted to be alone, but . . ."

"You're trying to tell me you're worried about me," I said.

There was a pause. "Pretty stupid, huh?" Bibi finally said.

Bibi was sitting on the edge with her legs in the water, just like a child. I swam to her, got out, pulled on a robe, and sat beside her, dangling my legs in the water alongside hers.

Bibi turned her head to look at me. I kept my eyes fixed on the water. "You sound okay," she said. "I mean, you know, like yourself."

"I am myself, Bibi," I answered quietly. "In all the ways that count."

"I would like to believe that," she said. "It's just . . . you let him do it. You let him make you a vampire."

"Sloane attacked me," I said. "He did exactly what he did to Randolph, except even worse. I thought my life was over, Bibi. I was literally moments away from death, and all I could think was that I didn't want to die. There were too many things I wanted to do. There still are. So I let Ash save me the only way he could. I let him make me a vampire."

I turned toward her, as if by holding her gaze I could make her understand. Make her do what I had done: view the world through new and different eyes.

"If you could have seen Ash that night . . . I know you would feel differently about him. The fact that he's a vampire doesn't mean he doesn't love me, Bibi. And whether you like it or not, can accept it or not, the truth is that Ash is the one great love of my life."

"That's quite a speech, Candace," she said after a moment.

"It was, wasn't it?" I said. "Sorry."

We each held out about ten seconds before we began to laugh.

"I can't believe it," Bibi gasped. "How in hell can we be laughing at a time like this?

"Candace," she suddenly said. "About what happened, when I came here the other night—"

"Oh, don't," I protested, cutting her off. "You've been my truest friend, Bibi. I've never doubted that, or you, not even for a moment."

"Well, shit," she said. "Now look what you've done. You've made me cry."

"Oh, no you don't," I said. And before I knew it, I had put an arm around her. She settled her head down onto my shoulder. For several silent moments we sat, just like that, arms around each other, our feet dangling in the satin water.

"You're going to do this, aren't you?" Bibi finally asked, her voice quiet. "You're going to go after Ash, to try and stop the Board."

"I have to," I answered. "The Board has to be stopped."

"And Ash?" Bibi asked.

"I can't leave him to be destroyed by them, Bibi. I love him too much."

She lifted up her head then, and I could see the conflicting emotions flickering in her eyes.

"*How?*" she burst out finally. "Honestly, I want to understand. But every time I try to fathom how you can know what Ash is, what he has to do to exist, and still love him, it's like running straight into a brick wall. I simply cannot comprehend how you can go on loving him."

"Of course you can," I said. "It's the same way you can say you love Randolph when you know he's married and never going to leave his rich wife. No, of course I don't equate the two of them," I said as I saw her stiffen. "What I'm saying is that love isn't just something that sneaks up on you without you realizing it or sweeps you away, though, if you're lucky, you get to feel those aspects of it.

"Love is a conscious, deliberate choice."

"That's just a little simplistic, don't you think?"

"No," I answered. "These days, I honestly don't. We've told ourselves that I've struggled against my feelings for Ash for two long years, Bibi. It isn't true. Somewhere along the line, I made a choice. A choice to keep on loving him.

"We tell ourselves the heart wants what it wants, that we can't control it, but that's just a convenient romantic lie. We choose our loves, Bibi. Second by second, minute by minute, day by day, year in and year out. If we're lucky, what we choose makes us happy. If we're not so lucky, it doesn't. Going after Ash now is just another point on the continuum. I'm still choosing love."

She was silent for so long, I thought she wasn't going to answer. But finally, she spoke.

"I really can't talk you out of this, can I?"

"No, you can't. If you love me, don't try to stop me."

She gave a quick, unamused laugh. "Now I know just how Carl felt. You don't fight fair, Candace."

"That's because I'm fighting to win," I said. "Fair doesn't always count. I have to finish this, Bibi. One way or the other."

"I don't know what to say to you," she said. "I really, truly don't."

"Tell me that you're still my friend," I said as, once again, I felt the tears begin to fill my eyes.

"Candace," a new voice said. "I think I've got something."

Bibi and I turned toward the sound. Chet was standing at the entrance to the grotto. I wiped tears from my cheeks with the backs of my hands. "What do you mean?"

"You know what?" Chet said. "I really, truly think I figured it out. The hieroglyphics were kind of unusual. I can explain upstairs. I don't want to bring the paper down here, and I think looking at it will help."

"We're on our way," I said. "Meet you in the study?"

"Great," Chet said.

Bibi stood up first. She held out a hand, pulled me up. Abruptly, the room swam and I swayed on my feet. Bibi's grip tightened.

"Candace, what is it?" she asked, her tone sharp with concern. "Are you all right?"

"Fine," I answered. A one-syllable lie. "I think I just stood up too quickly. That's all."

She peered down at me. "You don't look fine, if you don't mind my saying so."

"Thanks a lot," I said. I took a step and swayed once more, the weakness pulling at me like a riptide.

"You are *not* fine," Bibi declared as she put one arm around my back to steady me. "You're not fine at all. What is it? Is it Ash—that rapport thing again?"

I shook my head. "No." *It was the lack of him,* I realized. Without Ash's blood to sustain me, how long could I survive? "Honestly," I went on. "I'm all right. I'm just a little tired. That's all. Just help me get upstairs. Let's see what Chet has discovered."

And, I added silently, *let's hope that whatever strength I have left will be enough.*

Sixteen

"Okay, so," Chet said. The three of us were leaning over the desk in Ash's study. Chet was holding the magnifying glass over the Mark of Thoth. "When you take a really good look, you can see that what looks like just three hieroglyphs turns out to be a whole lot more. Each individual image is actually made up of many smaller hieroglyphs. My guess is that's why it didn't get translated before."

"But you figured it out," I said.

"I had help. I used a decoding program. It turns out the hieroglyphs were also a clever cipher. Once the computer figured out the pattern, I could eliminate all the hieroglyphs that had no meaning—a straight translation is total gobbledygook. There are actually only three distinct pictographs that matter. In order, I think they translate as Breath, Light, and Time." He shrugged. "The only problem is, I'm not sure how those concepts help us."

I sat down in the desk chair, aware of both Chet and Bibi's anxious eyes upon me. "To tell you the truth," I said, "I'm not sure I do, either. I'm also not sure that makes any difference. I still have to try and stop the Board."

"What if we just hide the paper somehow?" Bibi asked. "Try and buy some more time."

I shook my head. "You guys are forgetting what happened to Randolph. He had what the Board wanted, and they came and took it. If this is the third Emblem, they'll come for this, too. And they won't care about hurting anyone who gets in their way. If I go to them, at least I stop making the two of you targets."

"Maybe we don't want you to sacrifice yourself for our sakes," Bibi began.

"Stop," I said, holding up my hands for silence. "Just stop, both of you. I have to go. I have no choice."

Chet was silent for a moment, regarding me steadily. "When will you go?" he finally asked.

I ran a hand through my hair, suddenly realizing I had no idea what time it was. A thousand years seemed to have passed between the moment I'd been snatched away from Ash and this one.

"What time is it now?"

Chet consulted his high-tech watch. "About five a.m."

That ruled out "immediately," I thought. The sun was already up, and its power, its ability to sap what little strength I had was only going to get stronger as the day went on. Waiting until it was past its zenith, waiting at all, was a calculated risk, but one I would have to take. My only consolation was that not even Sloane would want to be out when the power of the sun was at its peak.

"I'll wait until the sun goes down," I answered, praying that neither Bibi nor Chet would see through the lie. I wouldn't wait nearly that long, but would set out as soon as the sun began its descent across the sky. Its power would still be strong, but it would be on the wane.

"Until then, I'll rest," I said. "Conserve my strength as best I can." I slid the paper with Ash's image on one side and the Mark of Thoth on the other toward me. "I think I'll study this a little more."

"We should stay with you," Bibi said.

I shook my head. "No, I think it's better if I'm alone. Being around humans is only going to get more difficult as time goes on."

"But," Chet began. Bibi reached out and laid a restraining hand on his arm. "Oh."

"We'll come back just before sundown," Bibi said.

"I'll be fine between now and then," I said. "I just need some time alone."

Silently, the three of us filed out of the study and headed for the front door. It was sort of like seeing guests out after the world's most miserable dinner party.

"Take care, Candace," Chet said as I opened the door.

"You, too," I said.

Chet moved off down the front walk, leaving Bibi and me alone.

"I refuse to blubber about this," she said.

"I should hope so," I said. "We've already blubbered quite enough. Go home and get some rest, Bibi. Then go visit Randolph. Do whatever you have to do to celebrate life."

"If you don't stop sounding like some therapy talk-show host, I'm not going to go at all." She threw her arms around me and held me close. "I'll see you tonight."

"Okay," I said. "But now you have to let go."

"I don't want to," she said. She gave me one last squeeze then stepped back. "It's harder than I thought."

"That makes two of us," I said. I made a shooing motion with my hands. "Go. Now."

She turned, walked halfway down the front walk, then turned back. "I'm coming back, Candace," she said in a calm, clear voice. "I'm coming back, and so are you."

Then she walked to the car without looking back. I waited until Chet's taillights had disappeared around the corner, then returned to the still and silent house, alone.

Seventeen

I waited until late afternoon, when the sun was just above the horizon line. The good news was that it was spring, not summer. The sun set sooner, and the daytime temperature was more moderate. Going outside was still not going to be precisely what I called fun, but I thought I could manage it.

Who the hell was I kidding? I didn't exactly have a choice.

I dressed in the bedroom Ash and I had once shared, feeling like David getting ready to face Goliath. A pair of sturdy stretch jeans, black T-shirt, a pair of light-trail hiking boots. I fastened on a waist pack, carefully folded the paper Ash and I believed might be the Tongue of Thoth, and placed it inside. I thought longingly about my silver stakes, all of which I'd had to give away, because they were now lethal to me as well as my enemies.

Finally, I grabbed two bottles of water from the fridge and put on a pair of shades. I went to the garage, started up Ash's car, and set off.

Panic gripped me hard. I knew I couldn't defeat Sloane and the Board. I doubted I could save Ash. I just knew I had to find him.

I had only a vague idea of where I was going. I was trusting in a flash of a pain-filled vision to guide me. *Fine, then I'll trust it,* I told myself. Somehow I would trust the psychic connection; the rapport between me and Ash would lead me to him.

The brief glimpse of Ash's surroundings that had come to me during that incredible moment of shared pain had convinced me that Sloane had taken Ash into the mountains. In many ways, the terrain outside Vegas would be the perfect place for the ritual the Board was about to perform. Though there were plenty of mainstream hiking trails, there was lots of isolated territory as well.

Since Ash's house was on the outskirts of the city, it took only about half an hour to reach the overlook that led to the hiking trails of Red Rock. I was sure these trails would lead to the uniquely shaped rocks I was looking for. I parked the car and got out to consider my options. I gazed at my surroundings—an expanse of massive red rock, broken by the occasional yucca or barrel cactus—then did a quick study of the trail map posted by the park service. Quickly, I chose the trail that seemed to lead to the most remote area. The very thought of forcing my body uphill on even the gentle slope in front of me made me ache with weariness. But there was no sense in stalling.

If I didn't go to the Board, they would come to me. Of that I had no doubt. And when they did, more people I cared about could get hurt.

I headed for the far end of the overlook where my chosen trail snaked up into the hills. I had gone all of about four steps when I heard the sound of an engine coming at high speed up the hill. A moment later, a car spun into the overlook, dirt and gravel shooting out from beneath the tires. The driver was out of the car almost before the engine was off.

"I knew it. I just knew it," Chet said, sprinting toward me. "What the hell do you think you're doing? Do you even know where you're going?"

"What the hell are *you* doing here?" I countered.

Chet gave me an impatient look. "I followed you, of course."

"Oh, no," I said. "Don't think for a moment I'm going to let you come along."

"And just how do you propose to stop me?" he asked. "You can't fool me, Candace. Your strength is already starting to fade. What happens if you can't make it on your own?"

"I'll make it," I said, my tone stubborn. "Please,

Chet. Don't try to come. If something were to happen . . ."

"I know you think I'm useless because I'm not all big and brawny," he began.

"Don't be stupid," I said. "It isn't that at all. And we're wasting time standing here arguing."

"I couldn't agree more," he said. "So let's go."

I opened my mouth to protest further, but Chet put a hand on my arm, halting the flow of whatever words I had left.

"I told you vampires took my best friend, Candace," he said quietly. "What I didn't tell you was that my best friend was also my wife."

"Chet, I'm so sorry. I—"

Chet interrupted me. "There was nothing, not one damned thing, that I could do to help her. So maybe I can help you now, even if it isn't what you want. You're not the only one with a grudge to settle. So you can just stop trying to talk me out of this. I'm coming with you whether you like it or not. Now tell me how you're going to find Ash."

"Okay," I said, understanding that I couldn't dissuade him, and suddenly incredibly grateful not to be alone. "I'm going to try and use rapport," I explained. "Ash's and mine. I don't think he'll seek me out voluntarily, but the fact that we connected involuntarily before—"

"Like a homing beacon," Chet said at once.

"Something like that." I nodded. "I won't try to use it until we have to leave the trail, though."

Again, Chet understood at once. "Conserving energy. That's smart." He moved beyond me then, striding several determined paces up the path before turning around.

"Well, come on," he said. "What are you waiting for?"

The marked trail climbed steadily. After no more than about fifteen minutes, I was exhausted. Chet walked in front, reaching back a hand now and then to tug me along.

The trail ended in a broad overlook that opened onto a vista of the range, more red rock stretching out ahead of us, black snowcapped peaks in the distance. Chet uncapped a water bottle and we each took a drink.

"Okay," I said. "This is where the marked trail ends. It's time to try the rapport. Be patient with me. This may take a minute."

I tried not to think that it might not work.

"I'm not going anywhere," Chet promised.

I turned away from the panoramic view and faced the mountains themselves. Then, eyes closed, I reached deep inside myself for the undead zone. I felt a cool quiet embrace me, an oasis in my desert of struggle and pain, and then I reached out.

Ash, I thought. *Let me feel you. Let me know that you're there. . . .*

And suddenly I could feel Ash's presence, like a faint sound. Music playing so distantly I had to strain my ears to hear. I turned my body in the direction I thought was right and, at once, the connection got a little stronger. I opened my eyes.

"He's this way," I said, and started to pull myself up the steep rock face.

The contact with Ash stayed steady, drawing me to him like a lodestone. I held on to it as if it were my lifeline, fighting through the haze of exhaustion and pain. Without Chet, I never would have made it at all. I managed to put one foot in front of the other, to inch up jagged outcroppings, all the time too drained to sense that our climb was about to become an ascent straight into Hell.

And then, without warning, we were standing on a small plateau, two enormous boulders like misshapen shoulders straight ahead of us.

My head felt thick and foggy. My hands were filthy and scratched. My legs had no feeling left in them at all, but I remained standing. I knew if I sat down, I would never be able to get back up.

"This is it," I said. "That's what I saw in my vision, those two boulders."

Chet gasped for air. "You're sure?"

I nodded.

"It doesn't look like there's space enough between them for any kind of opening," he said. "Why would they bring him here?"

"That's what I'm going to find out. I really think you should go back now, Chet."

He shook his head. "What are you, nuts? We are not having this conversation again, Candace, so you can just stop arguing. I'm in this to the very end."

"I see," a new voice said. "That means you're just in time."

And suddenly, horribly, Sloane was there. He seemed to rise straight up from out of the ground. Chet and I moved at once, rolling in opposite directions, as if we had coordinated our efforts ahead of time. I was on my hands and knees, desperately trying to get up, to turn around. The thought of Sloane attacking from behind filled me with blind panic.

Sloane dove for Chet. I saw the glint of silver as Chet reached in his pocket for a stake—one of my stakes. But Sloane was too fast. He kicked Chet's hand, sending the stake flying. It hit the rocky ground with a feeble *ping*.

Chet fought back, lunging at Sloane, brandishing a silver jackknife. The blade nicked Sloane's wrist, and I saw him grimace as the lethal metal scorched his skin. But the painful wound did not stop him. I ran to Chet's side, but Sloane tossed me away with one powerful blow. My head hit the ground so hard I probably blacked out for a moment. Dizzy and nauseated, I tried to stand and immediately crumpled to my knees. I watched helplessly as Sloane picked Chet up by the scruff of the neck and threw him to the ground. Then the vampire kneeled on top of him, knees in his stomach, his powerful hands pressing Chet's arms down into the dirt. It would have been difficult enough to throw off a strong man from that position. It was impossible to dislodge Sloane. Chet kicked his legs in a helpless attempt to free himself. I heard Sloane laugh, saw him bend his head, and then his teeth were in Chet's throat.

Chet uttered a wet, hoarse cry of pain and terror, his legs thrashing wildly now. Sloane tore at his throat like a rabid dog. Chet's whole body spasmed, frantically trying to throw Sloane off.

Sloane threw back his head, as if to savor the course of living blood through his body. The lower half of his face gleamed with Chet's blood. Chet gave a great heave, and suddenly Sloane was tumbling off, rolling to one side, and Chet sat up. His eyes, wide and glazed with pain and terror, gazed into mine. I saw his mouth work, as if desperately trying to relay a message.

Sloane rose straight up. His powerful wings lifted him high into the air before he swooped back down. Snatching Chet up, as if he weighed no more than a feather, he carried him aloft even as he fed on him once more. I felt a shower of moisture rain down on my upturned face, knew I had been bathed by my friend's blood. I heard Sloane give a great cry. And then a loud snap—the crack of Chet's neck breaking.

As Chet's body fell back to earth, I felt the darkness rise to take me and remembered nothing more.

Eighteen

When I opened my eyes I was lying on my back in some sort of cave. The light was dim but I could make out hard red stone above and beneath me. I was still in my clothes, but the waist pack was gone.

My face itched. Experimentally, I brought my fingers to my face and discovered it was spattered with small, dry drops.

Chet's blood.

With a choked cry, I sat up. I was in a small room that can really only be described as a cell. The only entrance or exit was barred. A single candle burned in a sconce on the wall.

I wasn't alone.

In the far corner, where the light of the candle didn't quite reach, I could just make out a prone form. My heart in my throat, I crawled toward it.

"Ash," I sobbed.

He moved then, his hand reaching a fraction of an inch. I caught it, pressed it between both of mine.

Ash's skin was almost as cold as the stone floor. He was stripped to the waist. Even in the dim light, I could see the bruises along his face and torso.

I did this, I thought, sick with regret. If Ash hadn't been sustaining me with his blood, he would have healed. He had used his strength to save me and not kept enough for himself. *Did you even fight?* I wondered? Or had he fought too hard? Had he done his best to make them hurt him, believing that his end would bring about my freedom?

"Oh, Jesus," I whispered. "Ash, what have we done?"

"Candace," I heard his voice say then, no more than the thinnest of sounds. "Candace?"

"I'm here, Ash," I said.

He began to cough then, a horrible wet sound. *He is injured beyond repair,* I thought. Because of me, because of our love. If I could have given my life outright for his at that moment, I would have done it without a second thought.

"Candace," he said again, and he opened those eyes that I so loved. They were still the same, burning through the darkness as clear and pure as the light of the stars. He turned his hand within mine, lifting it toward my face.

"It *is* you," he said, and I heard the strange combination of joy and anguish in his voice. "Ah, God,

Candace, you shouldn't have come. You don't understand."

"Actually, I do," I said.

He made a move as if to sit up then, and I helped him upright. He propped himself up against the wall of the cell, head downcast, knees bent to support his arms. I sat facing him, my own arms around my knees, our legs touching. I was almost afraid to hold him in my arms. If I did, I would begin to weep, and I wanted to be strong.

"I know what will happen if you no longer exist, Ash," I said quietly. "I even forgive you for not telling me yourself."

His head jerked up. "But how?" Then he closed his eyes as the obvious truth occurred. "Sloane."

"Guess he just figured the information was too good not to share," I said. "It actually turned out to be useful to let him think I was so angry I would betray you. It would have worked, too, if Chet and Carl hadn't shown up. They thought they were saving me from the bad guy."

"So that's what happened." Ash opened his eyes, and his starlit gaze found mine. "You should have stayed away, Candace," he went on, his tone anguished. "What happens to me isn't important now. But believing you would be safe, be whole again . . . it's all that's kept me sane."

I leaned forward and then I did take him into my arms.

"Did you really think that I would turn my back on you?" I asked. "That I would buy back being human at such a terrible price? There is nothing in the world more important to me than you, Ash. Not even being human once more. If you think I would leave you alone to face whatever it is the Board is about to do, you love some other Candace."

He ran his fingertips across my face, wet with tears I'd shed after all. "No," he said, simply. "I know. That's why I didn't tell you. I knew you wouldn't let me make the ultimate sacrifice."

We sat for a moment, simply holding each other. "Chet translated the hieroglyphics," I said. "I know what they mean now. Not that I can see how it will do any good."

"But how?"

"It was a cipher. Chet was able to decode it with a computer program. Only three of the hieroglyphics have meaning: Breath, Light, Time. But it doesn't matter now. Poor Chet followed me here. Sloane killed him for it, and now the Board has all three Emblems."

"Then it's over," Ash said. I felt his arms tighten. "God, Candace. You shouldn't have come!"

"We belong together, Ash," I said. "Even if all we do together is die. I'm here because being with you is what I want, no matter what comes."

"Now this is what I call touching." Sloane's voice slid into the room.

I didn't turn to face him. I felt Ash stiffen and heard a clang as Sloane pushed open the door to the cell.

"You got him to sit up, I see," Sloane said with a sneer. "Congratulations. It's more than he would do for me."

I did turn then, moving to sit beside Ash, linking my arm through one of his.

"I'm glad you decided to join us, Candace," Sloane went on. His tone was conversational, but I could hear the undisguised triumph in his voice. "It gives me the opportunity to thank you in person for giving me everything I ever wanted. Because of you, Ash failed the Board's trials. And it was you who finally delivered him into my hands, however unintentionally.

"And now you've brought me the best gift of all: the Tongue of Thoth. The Chairman has confirmed that's what it is, by the way. He and the others will be here before the night is out. We'll complete the ritual—Ash will serve as the sacrifice—and then we'll have what we've sought. Immortality."

I waited for Sloane's words to move me to anger, to desperation or fear. Instead, I felt nothing, nothing at all. What he could do to Ash and me, what he would do, no longer felt important. All that was important was that Ash and I would be together at the end. I had been true to myself, my choice, my love.

"Do you like opera, Sloane?" I suddenly inquired. I felt a tremor move through Ash, knew he understood what I was trying to say. *Oh, how I love you, Ash,* I thought. No one else had ever been so quick, so in tune with every part of me. Body, heart, mind.

"What the hell is that supposed to mean?" Sloane demanded, and suddenly I could hear the uncertainty in his voice. Whatever reaction he had hoped to elicit from me or Ash, this wasn't it.

"Simple. It's not over till the fat lady sings," I said. "You're not immortal yet, Sloane."

He took a step toward us then, and I felt Ash's grip tighten on mine.

"Do you know the first thing I will do when I am immortal, Candace?" Sloane said. "The first thing I will do is take you out of this world. I don't even want you for a drone. Ash won't be able to save you. Not this time. He'll go to his end knowing that your blood is mine. You'll beg for mercy before the end, I promise you that."

"And we all know what your promises are worth, don't we?" I said as calmly as I could.

Sloane took an involuntary step forward. In the confines of the cell, he seemed enormous. I could see him fighting for control, his desire to destroy us both a palpable presence in the room.

"We'll see about that smart mouth of yours when the Chairman arrives," he said at last. "Enjoy your last moments together. They won't last long."

Without another word, he pivoted on one heel and strode out. The door clanged shut behind him. Silence filled the cell.

"I pegged that asshole the moment I met him," I said. "Hollywood vampire. He doesn't even have any original lines."

Ash laughed then, the sound open and surprised. And suddenly, I knew that even if Sloane made good on every single threat, even if I begged and wept before he took my life, it would be worth it. Even in this dark and death-filled place, I had brought my lover joy, just one last time.

"There is something I want you to know," I said, and felt Ash's arms tighten.

"Hush, Candace," he said. "No more words now."

"Just these," I said. "I know that we are both about to die. And I want you to know that I love you. Our love is the great surprise of my life. My only regret is that I didn't understand sooner. I should have accepted all you had to offer long ago.

"If I could become a true vampire now, I would do it. I would drink living blood so that we could be together for all time."

I felt his body tremble then, whether with grief or joy I could not tell.

"Love me, Ash," I said. "Let me love you, let me choose you, one last time."

"As I choose you, Candace," he said. "Now and forever."

"Now and forever," I echoed.

And then our lips spoke not in words but in a language that would outlast time. In that cold and terrible place, Ash and I made love as we never had before. Sweetly and simply. Every touch, every gesture, an undying pledge. No matter what happened to either of us before the end, nothing the Board could do, nothing in the heavens or on earth, could take away our choice, our love. And as I felt Ash fill me, as I took him deep inside my body for the very last time, it seemed to me that I felt our love rise up, slip the boundaries of our bodies to take on a life of its own. A life that would remain, that would endure, when our own lives were done.

Now and forever, I thought as I felt us, together,

quiver on the edge of desire, burst through, then begin the long slide down. *Forever and now.*

Until even time itself was spent, and the stars, like the light of Ash's eyes, went out across the skies one by one.

Nineteen

All too soon, Sloane came back for us. And this time, he wasn't alone. He had several low-level vampires with him, all with the Mark of Thoth on their bare chests, the sign of their allegiance to the Board.

"Separate them," Sloane said.

Two of the vampires pulled me away as others hauled Ash to his feet. Then, before I realized his intention, Sloane stepped to Ash, raised a fist, and struck him back down. Ash dropped to his knees, the bones slapping, hard, against the stone. I strained against the arms that held me.

"Bastard," I cried. "You filthy fucking bastard."

Sloane turned to me with a brilliant smile. "I could be a little nicer, but you'll have to beg me for it."

"I hope you spend your immortality in Hell."

"Not a bad idea," Sloane said sweetly. "Except that I've developed a taste for blood. I think an eternal existence among a sea of potential living victims will be so much more rewarding, don't you?"

He gave a flick of his fingers, his false pleasantness vanishing as if turned off by a switch. The low-level vampires beside Ash hauled him to his feet once more.

"Take him to the altar," he commanded. "Bring her and hold her until the Chairman comes."

The main cavern looked as if it had been taken straight out of ancient Egypt. A fine layer of golden sand whispered softly underfoot. Draperies of sheer linen shot with gold thread looped down from the ceiling, concealing the stalactites above. Torches cast flickering light from sconces along the walls. Incense burners filled the air with a sweet yet smoky scent.

At the cavern's far end was a great, flat stone on a raised dais. Behind it, an enormous statue of the god Thoth, made entirely of beaten gold except for its eyes. They were rubies. *Red for blood,* I thought. And like most ancient rituals, this one would demand a blood sacrifice.

Sloane's vampire henchmen dragged Ash to the altar and shoved him down on his back. From beneath it, they pulled thin straps of leather, which they used to lash him to the altar. Ash made no attempt to struggle but lay quietly. His only action was to turn his head, his silver eyes searching the cavern until they found mine. All I could do was stand, my arms imprisoned in the tight grip of my captors, my eyes on Ash's, and wait for what would come.

I didn't have to wait very long.

Utterly without warning, the first of the Board members appeared in the air above our heads, his great wings beating the air, then folding as he settled slowly to the ground. A strange humming seemed to fill the air. Not one made by the low-level vampires ringing the walls around me. This was utterly inhuman. As if the very air itself was seething with energy, giving off its own sound.

One by one, the other Board members materialized as the first one had. Each moved to take his place, flanking the statue of Thoth on either side. Sloane stepped into position. There were six Board members present now. Only one was still missing: the Chairman.

And then, quite suddenly, he was there. Bursting into view overhead, his great wings seeming to fill the entire cavern they stretched so wide. The humming tension in the air rose to a shriek then ended abruptly. Absolute silence filled the chamber, a silence broken only by the sound of the Chairman's great wings. They beat once, twice. Then, with a sound like a sigh, he furled them, gathering them into his body in a single fluid motion as he settled lightly to the ground. He stood for a moment, surveying the scene. He turned his head, and I saw his face for the very first time.

Oh, but he is so beautiful, I thought. The most terrible beauty that I had ever seen. His face was smooth, unlined. But his eyes were ancient, filled with time-old malice, age-old shattered dreams and hopes. More than anything in the world, what I wanted in that moment was to close my eyes. But I kept my gaze steady on his even as he walked straight toward me.

"So," he said, in a voice to match his face. Deep and musical, and somehow many voices all at once. "This is the human woman who has been the cause of so much trouble. Candace, isn't it?"

Somehow, I found my voice. "Candace Steele," I said, succinctly.

The Chairman smiled, a smile that did not reach his eyes. Before I realized what he intended, he reached out with one hand to capture my face, turning it from side to side. The skin on my face crawled. His fingers burned, a combination of fire and ice.

"Such a pity," the Chairman said. "Not only are

you lovely, but you have great strength. You would have made a fine vampire. But very soon now, I'm afraid you will be nothing at all. You should have chosen your passions with greater care."

He released me then, the imprint of his fingers still burning my skin. The Chairman turned and strode straight to the great stone table where Ash was bound. For many moments, he simply stood, gazing down. Ash gazed back. A great blanket of silence filled the cavern.

"And you," the Chairman said, addressing Ash, and for the first time, I thought I detected something genuine, something almost human in his voice. Regret, perhaps? "You are the greatest waste of all. You could have been so much. You could have *had* so much. Now, you will have nothing. You will be nothing."

"You're wrong," Ash said in a quiet voice. "I will be what I have always been: myself."

"And what are you, Ash?" the Chairman taunted. There was nothing but fury in his voice now. "You are a prisoner. Soon, you will be a sacrifice. We will reunite the Emblems of Thoth, restore the power of the god—a power that will flow through you. And when it does, we will feed upon you. We will take the god's power into us and become immortals. You will be destroyed. At the end, you will no longer be yourself. You'll be nothing but a conduit for the power of the god."

"At least I'll be free of you," Ash said.

The Chairman struck him, full across the face. A blow that drew blood. He reached down, ran his fingers brutally across Ash's face, digging his nails into the skin, then strode to the statue of the god. Raising his hand, he placed it on Thoth's chest, directly over the great god's heart. Then he drew back, the imprint of his bloody hand plainly visible on the gold.

"Let it begin," he said. "And let it end with that which has sustained us."

From around the chamber, the Board members gave back the word that would commence the ritual:

"Blood."

The ritual for immortality began in earnest then, all the more terrifying because, following that initial incantation, it was performed in almost total silence. The Chairman had begun his twisted existence with a curse upon his tongue. So now, the ritual that would free him and his followers would be performed in silence. Until the ritual was complete, the god reunited with the Emblems of his power, the members of the Board would utter no sound.

One by one, the Board members followed the Chairman's example, wiping their hands in Ash's blood and anointing the statue of Thoth. Last of all was the Board's newest member, Sloane. He struck Ash, as the Chairman had. And then a second time, when his first blow failed to draw Ash's now sluggish blood. He did not speak as he drew his hand across Ash's face, but his face told his thoughts clearly enough.

After two long years, Sloane's triumph was almost complete. His competition with Ash, almost over and done. From now until the end of time he would be free to do evil with no possibility of destruction. Nothing would ever be able to stop him or the rest of the Board.

Sloane placed his handprint upon the others then stepped back, and I realized that I was weeping, silently. The six Board members stood in a semicircle, facing Thoth's statue. The Chairman, directly in front of the god. Still in silence, he held out a hand. Into it, Sloane placed the heart scarab, the Heart of Thoth. The Board members knelt, their hands uplifted, palms up, as if in supplication. The Chairman reached up and pressed the scarab against the statue, directly over the bloody handprints.

I felt a strange vibration then, coming up

through the soles of my feet, as if power had begun to flow into the room from the very bowels of the earth itself. Against the burnished gold statue, the green heart scarab seemed to glow. The gold statue now took on a strange and liquid sheen, almost as if it were growing warm. Sweat broke out on Ash's body, seeming to mirror the statue's response. Then, as if it had come to life, I saw the beetle spread its wings, flex its legs. The Board members brought their hands together sharply, just once, and the vibration stopped.

The Emblem was true. The first part of the god's power had been restored.

Now, from around his own neck, the Chairman drew a great gold chain. At the end of it dangled a golden disc, resting in a crescent also made of gold. It was an exact representation of Thoth's headdress. *The Body of Thoth,* I thought. The Chairman turned back to Ash, took the Emblem and pressed it against Ash's forehead. Ash gave a choked cry. When the Chairman lifted the Emblem, I could see its outline etched into Ash's skin, the outline oozing blood.

Then, his great wings unfurling, the Chairman rose straight up, hovering in the air before the face of the god. He pressed the Emblem into Thoth's forehead, as he had pressed it to Ash's. Below him, his followers brought their hands together a second time. The clap resounded through the chamber. The linen hangings moved in an unseen wind. The gold of the statue seemed to ripple, as if with muscles coming to life. Ash's body jerked and spasmed, straining against his leather bindings, utterly beyond his ability to control.

Slowly, slowly, the Chairman returned to earth. The second his feet touched the floor of the cavern, Sloane was at his side. In his hand, he held a rolled piece of paper, and I thought my heart would break. For this was the paper I had brought with me, the paper with the hieroglyphics Chet had translated. The third, the final Emblem. This was the Tongue of Thoth.

And now the Chairman did speak as he approached the statue of the god for the third, the final, time.

"Great God," he said in his multihued voice. "Thoth of powerful magic, hear now the plea of your most faithful follower. Once, in my vanity, I displeased you. I overstepped my bounds. And for this, you punished me, condemned me and all those who followed me to an existence neither living nor dead.

"But we have remained true to your magic. We have not forsaken you, great God. Reward us now.

We bring you a sacrifice, to feed you. We reunite you with the Emblems of your great power. We beseech you, grant us the gift that we long for."

The Chairman reached up. And I saw that his hand trembled as he placed the Tongue of Thoth into the statue's upraised right hand.

"Make us immortal."

The Board members brought their hands together for the third and final time. The sound of flesh against flesh resounded through the chamber as, this time, the Chairman joined them. I felt a jolt of energy, like a surge of electricity, and thought I understood. The Chairman and his fellow Board members were linked now. Their bodies still separate but their power as one. They knelt in the shape of a great V, with the Chairman as the point, then raised their hands above their heads, palms facing the statue of the god. The air in the chamber grew thick with heat.

The Chairman is the focal point, I thought. *What happens to him will happen to them all.*

"Hear us, great god!" the Chairman called out. "Grant us the gift that we long for, we beg you. Make us immortal!"

Nothing happened.

Nothing at all.

Ash began to laugh then. From somewhere

within his battered body, he produced a deep, luxurious sound. It rolled through the room like a breaker on a smooth beach.

And then, suddenly, Sloane was there. Leaping up from his knees, raising his fist, then striking Ash again and again. His mouth moved in furious words, but the sound of Ash's laughter drowned them out. I began to struggle fiercely with my captors, desperate to reach Ash's side. It was futile. Sloane's open hand slashed down again, whipping Ash's head to one side. Even as Ash's laughter ceased, his eyes looked straight into mine.

I stopped struggling abruptly, not even feeling the pain as my captors forced me down. Because, in that moment, Ash was with me. Once more I felt the thread of our rapport. Thin as a spider's web, but also as strong. And into my mind there came a single question, as if Ash had planted it there.

How did Thoth create himself?

I made a strangled sound. Because I understood then, and wondered if Ash had known all along what would happen. Understood that the Chairman would never see it, because of his own past, the curse he had borne for time out of mind. Thoth's most powerful act of magic had been his own manifestation in the world. He had brought himself into being by speaking his own name.

By speaking aloud.

"*You can turn this on them,*" Ash said inside me.

Sloane was shaking an inert Ash, screaming now. The other Board members surged to their feet to seize him, pulling him away from the altar. *They don't want him to kill Ash until the moment is right,* I realized. As it was, Ash wouldn't last much longer. Blood dripped down his face. He gave a sudden cough, and I saw the way it bloomed from inside his mouth. *Spent, he is almost spent,* I thought.

"*Do it, Candace,*" I heard him say inside my head. "*Say the words. The power of the ritual will become yours. Speak, and you will destroy them.*"

"*But I'll destroy you, as well,*" I thought. "*There must be a sacrifice. The ritual demands it.*"

"*And there will be a sacrifice,*" Ash replied. "*Candace, my Candace. Trust me. Say the words. Love me forever, as I love you. Let go of your fear. Let me go.*"

I began to sob in earnest then. For here, at last, there was no way out. I could stop the Board, give Ash the last gift he would ever ask for. I could stop his enemies. All I had to do was the one thing I couldn't do: I had to let Ash go.

I swallowed, feeling every single muscle in my throat. And then I lifted up my voice.

"Breath," I said aloud.

At once, a cool wind swept through the cavern. The linen hangings swayed. The torches flickered, wildly. The Chairman was on his feet now. Moving toward Ash, but his eyes were on me.

"Light."

There was a clap of thunder, and the whole cavern swayed. Chunks of rocks came crashing down. Crying out in fear, my vampire captors abandoned me, fleeing for the safety of the far reaches of the cave. Then, with a great groan, a large crack appeared on the cave's roof, wide enough to reveal a full moon floating in a cloudless sky.

"She is doing it!" the Chairman cried. "The woman is completing the ritual."

"Not yet," Ash said. *"Wait."*

"Don't be a fool," Sloane snarled. "She'll never betray Donahue. It's some sort of trap. Stop her. Destroy her now while there's still time."

But there is no time left, Sloane, I thought. *Not for you. Not for the Board.* I looked into his horrified, desperate eyes and smiled.

"Now!" Ash said.

"Time," I said aloud.

For a moment, just as had been the case for the Chairman, nothing happened. Nothing at all. Then the walls of the cavern began to tremble. The moonlight grew impossibly bright. And then a single ray of light shot down, straight onto the head of the statue of Thoth. It struck the golden headdress, and a second ray of light branched out from the first, this one illuminating Ash's captive form. I felt a sudden surge of energy, incredible in strength, impossible to describe. As if everything that had ever happened in all the world was running through my veins at once, and with it, all the possibilities for every single moment still to come.

"See!" I heard the Chairman cry. "See, it is the power of the god!"

I felt Ash's body spasm upward, suddenly filled to the brim with unimaginable power. Then, as if a circuit breaker had been tripped inside my brain, our rapport snapped off. I saw the Chairman surging toward Ash, desperate to feed, to draw the power of the god into himself. He stepped into the ray of light.

And was caught in the web of time.

With a horrible scream, the Chairman stopped short, immobilized by the light. Around him, the other Board members froze as well. Linked to the Chairman, all were held captive by the revitalized power of Thoth. A power that now made them prisoners of a power even greater than the god's own. The power of time.

For one crystalline moment, the Chairman's astonishing beauty shone forth. Never, or so it seemed to me, could he have been as beautiful as he was at that moment, the end of his long span of time. And I realized that I could see right through him, as if his body had become a thin cotton handkerchief with his image stamped upon it. I felt the wind return then, no more than the briefest flutter of air. But it was enough. The image of the Chairman rippled, then wavered. And then the wind sighed through it as the Chairman and all his followers crumbled into dust. I saw them fall through the air, as if in slow motion, even as the light grew so bright I had to shield my eyes. The last thing I saw was the great golden image of Thoth, standing over Ash's motionless form.

When I opened my eyes once more, I was alone. The cavern was empty. The statue of Thoth was gone. I staggered to my feet, stumbled to the altar where Ash had been held captive. The leather straps were still in place, their knots still tightly tied. I could just make out the outline of where Ash had lain, as if his form had literally been etched into the stone by the strength of the light.

I stared at the empty altar, feeling my own heart shatter. Ash was gone. He had disappeared. As utterly and completely as the Chairman and his Board.

I climbed onto the stone, fit myself within the confines of the outline of his body, and wept. I was still there when the sun rose and I discovered I was human once more.

Twenty

Several days later, I stood at Chet's grave, Al on one side, and Bibi on the other. With us stood various other staff members from the Scheherazade. Chet had no family. The group of friends who had assembled to honor his life was small. But I knew all those present would miss him. I would miss him, and I would do my best to honor his memory with my own actions. Though only Bibi and I knew it, Chet had given his life for mine.

My life, which I would never take for granted again. Not that I had for a good, long while. But unlike literally anyone else I knew, I had firsthand experience of at least some of what lay beyond. I had been both more than human, and less.

I wasn't quite sure what that made me now.

The minister finished the quiet words of the ceremony. Chet's coffin was lowered into the ground. Al stepped forward to cast the first handful of earth upon the dark, glossy wood. Then Chet's other co-workers from the Sher did the same, one by one.

I went last, gathering up a handful of earth, stepping to the edge of Chet's grave until my toes extended into space. I reached out my arm. But then, for what seemed like endless moments, I could not make my hand open. Instead, my fist stayed clenched tight. As if I could not quite bring myself to perform this last act. To admit that Chet was well and truly gone.

"Candace?" I heard Bibi's quiet voice say, heard the worry in her tone. And as though the sound of her voice had broken a spell, I opened my hand and let the earth fall. It landed on Chet's coffin with a sound like rain.

Good-bye, Chet, I thought. *Thank you for being my true friend. Thank you for my life.*

I've never been big on trying to figure out what the dead would have wanted, and then acting accordingly. Too many gray areas where self-indulgence and self-deception can roam. But in Chet's case I had to figure it was pretty much a no-brainer. Vampires had taken him; they'd taken his wife.

I'll continue the fight, I vowed silently. *Our fight.* Being a vampire briefly hadn't made me think they were the good guys. An eye for an eye. Blood for blood. A life for a life. Chet would have wanted me to do what he'd tried to do himself. Take the vampires out of the equation, even the score.

Arm in arm, Bibi and I stepped away from the

grave and began to walk across the freshly clipped grass toward where we'd parked our cars. Al stayed behind, talking to the minister.

"Look," Bibi said suddenly. "There's Carl."

I hadn't heard from Carl Hagen in the days since Chet's death, since I had staggered down the mountain. The police had questions regarding the hiking accident that was listed as Chet's official cause of death. Carl hadn't posed them.

But my own condition—severe dehydration, a variety of cuts, bruises, and scrapes—had convinced the detective who interviewed me that no foul play had been involved. Chet McGuire had met with an unfortunate accident. I was lucky to be alive. As to the third member of our party, Ashford Donahue III, his body had yet to be found. After several futile days of combing the area where Chet's body was recovered, the police had reluctantly called off the search.

I knew Carl still had questions. He was too smart a man, too good a cop, not to. I also knew him well enough to know the breathing space he'd given me was only postponing the inevitable. Sooner or later, the day of reckoning between us would come. But he'd held off so far, and for that, I was grateful.

"You should talk to him," Bibi said. "He's called every day to make sure you're all right."

In the days since the accident, I had been staying with Bibi. My own house was still undergoing repairs.

"Okay," I said, not seeing any way around it.

"I'll have a pot of coffee ready when you get back to my place," she promised.

"Bibi." I made a spontaneous decision. Actually not so spontaneous. It was something I'd been thinking about since coming down from the mountains. "I'll stop by and get my stuff, but then I need to go to Ash's house. I want to stay there for a while—at least until my own place is ready."

"Why?" she asked bluntly. "Isn't that a little like rubbing salt into a wound?"

"Maybe," I admitted. "But I need to face it. It's the only way I'll move on."

"Are you sure you're ready?" she asked. "You're sure you'll be all right on your own?"

I won't be on my own, I thought. *I think about Ash, every minute.*

"I'm sure," I replied. "I have to go back there sooner or later. You know me: When in doubt, meet things head-on." I gave her a quick hug. "Now stop worrying. I'll be fine."

"Okay," Bibi said. I saw her focus shift. "Hello, Carl."

"Hi, Bibi," Carl said. His gaze flicked to me. "Steele. I'm glad you're still alive."

"That makes two of us," I said. "It was good of you to come, Carl."

Something in his expression lightened. "Thanks," he said. "I wanted to, I just . . . we didn't part on the best of terms. I didn't want to intrude."

"You didn't," Bibi said swiftly. "Not at all." She stepped away, moving toward her car. "I'll talk to you tonight, Candace."

"Okay," I said. Carl and I were left alone.

"You doing okay?" he asked after a moment.

"For the most part," I said. "It's going to take some time, Carl."

"Sure, that figures," he said. "I'm pretty good at waiting."

I gave a smile, as I thought he'd intended me to. "I know."

"How soon are you going back to work?" he asked.

"To tell you the truth, I don't know. Al's being really great about cutting me a lot of slack. We're going to talk about it some more next week."

"If you need a place to stay," Carl went on, his tone slightly awkward now. "I've got that spare room."

"You mean the one filled with fishing tackle?" I asked, and won a smile of my own. "I think I'll pass, but I appreciate the thought." I hesitated for a moment, then decided the truth was best. "Actually, I'm going to stay at Ash's place until mine is fixed up."

"I see," Carl said. He took a breath then added, "I'd like to call you, if that's all right."

I put my arms around him in a spontaneous hug. *So warm,* I thought. *So solid.*

"Of course it's all right. Is Tuesday still your day off?" I asked.

He nodded. "Outstanding," I said. "I'll call you, and you can take me to dinner. How does that sound?"

"Like I just walked straight into that one," Carl said.

"That would be because you did," I replied as I got into Ash's car. "I'll see you Tuesday, Carl."

Carl was still standing at the edge of the grass, the headstones in tidy rows at his back, as I pulled out of the graveyard and headed for Ash's house.

Late that night, I lay awake in the bed Ash and I had once shared, listening to the beat of my own heart. Its sound filled my head, moved outward from my body until it seemed to fill the entire house. Ash was dead; I was alive. For as long as my heart beat, those two facts would be inextricably entwined. The very rhythm of my heart pounding out a song to life with one beat, with the next, a hymn of loss.

I don't know how to bear this, I thought. *I don't know how to live without you, Ash.*

Finally, unable to stand the bed any longer, the scent of Ash's skin clinging faintly to the sheets, I got up and roamed the house.

I walked to the living room, moving to stand before one of the big, picture windows. Leaning against the cold glass, I gazed up at the stars. The stars that would always remind me of Ash's eyes, just as they had from the very first night. And suddenly, my own eyes were filled with tears, the first I had shed since becoming human once more. That most human of feelings, regret, seemed to fill every cell of my body, and I wondered if I would spend the rest of my life wishing I could go back, be given a second chance. Start over.

I'm sorry, Ash, I thought. *Sorry I didn't see the truth of what I wanted sooner.* If I had, would he be with me now? If I had become a true vampire the night of Sloane's attack, would we have been strong enough to defeat the Board together without either one of us paying such a terrible price?

Stop it, I told myself sharply. This was not doing me any good. In fact, it seemed a straight road to a complete and utter breakdown.

You can get through this, not just because you have to, but because it's what you want. Ash wanted you to live. You want to live. There's no time like the present.

Love him forever, but get on with your life. Stop screwing around.

And in that moment, I could have sworn I heard Ash laugh, felt the brush of his thoughts against my mind, his pleasure at my strength. I drew in my first breath of peace. For the first time believing that, even if I could not see the way yet, somehow, I would go on. *You're giving me this, too, aren't you, Ash?* I thought. *Not just life but the will to live it.*

I turned away from the window, then cried out as my bare feet encountered something I knew had not been there before. Scattered across the wood of the living room floor, trailing off down the hall like a path of polished shells.

Sweet pea blossoms.

"Ash," I whispered, as my heart did a great leap into my throat. Only Ash knew my love for this particular flower. "Ash!" I said, more urgently now.

Around me, the house stayed silent. But, as if in answer, the scent of the blossoms rose up. I knelt, scooped up a handful, and brought them to my face and, as I did, I swear I felt Ash's presence for a second time.

You're here, aren't you? I thought.

Now and forever. That's how long we had sworn

our love would last. Forever and now. Ash had not let go of me any more than I had let go of him. Somewhere, somehow, what he was lived on.

I gazed down at the blossoms, shimmering in my hand. *White, for mourning,* I thought. *White, for hope.*

I walked to the front door, pulled it open, stepped out onto the walk. And then I flung the blossoms as hard and high as I could. High enough to reach the stars.

Can't get enough Vegas vampire vixen?

Don't miss the Candace Steele book
that started it all!
Turn the page to catch a sneak peak at

Passionate Thirst

The first book in the
Candace Steele Vampire Killer series
by Cameron Dean!

Prologue

He was the sexiest guy I had seen in Vegas.

Considering how many guys I see in a day, that's saying something.

Not only that, I see all kinds, from sleek high-rollers in silk shirts and Italian leather shoes, wreathed in clouds of expensive cologne, to slobs in Hawaiian shirts and flip-flops, oozing bad body odor. As a general rule, casinos don't get terribly exercised about dress codes. Most don't care too much about what you've got on, or what you don't, as long as you can make it through the door to lay your money down. For a guy to make me sit up and take notice like this one did, he had to really be something special.

Trust me, he was.

Though mentioning sitting up is slightly mislead-ing as I was on my feet at the time, and they hurt. But then they usually do. Occupational hazard of my job. I'm on my feet, my high-heeled feet, a good eight hours a day, cocktail waitressing at Vegas's newest mega-casino, the Scheherazade. One of the first things you learn: Do not, under any circumstances, take off your shoes till you go off-shift, no matter how much you might want to.

After shift, however, you can take off anything your little heart desires. Which brings me back to the guy.

"It's so unfair," my co-worker, Marlene, moaned as we shared a rare moment of togetherness while waiting for our drink orders. In our regulation high heels, gauzy harem pants, and pillbox hats, I figure we looked like two *I Dream of Jeannie* clones, Vegas style, though I think even Jeannie would have drawn the line at the pink velour halter tops.

"Who shows up in my section?" she went on. "Guys who look like Beavis or Butt-Head. You get Sean Connery as James Bond."

It was a good description, I had to admit. The male in question was currently at the blackjack table I covered, looking like he owned the place and winning like there was no tomorrow. I spotted him as soon as I came back on the floor from my mid-shift break. Tall, dark, and handsome with a sort of lean and rangy build that kept him from sliding too far into *GQ* territory. Though his clothing was plainly expensive, charcoal-colored pants and a white cotton shirt so sheer I could almost see right through it, he didn't look as if he had been born with a silver spoon in his mouth. Instead he looked . . . hungry. An alpha male wolf in designer clothing. As combinations go, it packed quite a punch.

Down, girl. You're still on the clock, I thought.

I have very strict personal rules about tangling up the sheets with casino patrons, a thing my co-workers know quite well. Going to bed with strangers may sound exciting. And it is, sometimes. But a girl gets tired of being the thing that happens in Vegas and stays in Vegas.

Marlene has a good ten years on my twenty-something, all of which she's spent happily married to her high school sweetheart, a guy with a face so gorgeous it almost has me convinced angels really do walk among us. She was about as likely to take a roll with a customer as she was to flap her arms and fly to Mars.

"You're tempted. Admit it, Candace. Please, please tell me you're going to cut loose just this once. If you don't, Gloria will get him and we'll all have our noses rubbed in it for weeks."

Gloria, a stacked blond who staffed one of the roulette wheels, was a notorious man-eater of the kiss-and-tell variety.

"Well," I said slowly, no longer making any attempt to hold back the smile. The truth was, I *was* tempted. Very. In a way I hadn't been in quite some time. "He *is* pretty spectacular. And I guess there's not much point in having rules if you don't break them every once in a while."

Marlene gave a whoop of triumphant laughter. "Now you're talking. Have I ever mentioned one of the things I like best about you is your sense of . . . proportion?"

"Oh, now you're just talking dirty," I chastised.

She leaned toward me, lowering her voice conspiratorially. "Let Mama Marlene give you one little tip. Do absolutely everything I wouldn't do. And for future reference, always remember that Butt-Head is the ugly one."

I was laughing as I plunged into the crowd.

" 'Night, James," I said to the employee entrance doorman four hours later. I was now officially off the clock.

" 'Night, yourself, Candace," he said, his voice like ground gravel. "Don't do anything I wouldn't do, now."

"Wouldn't think of it," I said, and earned a smile.

Cutting around the side of the building, I headed

for the Strip. The truth is, I love Vegas at night. Sure it's loud and bright and phony. It's also vibrant, colorful, *alive*. The truth is, I've never seen a place more dedicated to the future than Vegas is. Even the air seems filled with a sense of anticipation. Because the thing about gambling is that you can never quite predict the outcome.

I heard a car horn honk, a voice call out, and I lifted my hand in greeting as one of the city's numerous cabs shot by. Tourists almost never realize this, but there's actually a strong connection among the locals in this town. So many faces coming and going, you get so you notice the ones who stay put. I paused in front of the Bellagio, watching the way the lights flirted with the waters of the fountain.

"That's the first time I've ever seen anybody do that," a voice behind me said.

I felt a cool shiver of anticipation slide straight down my spine. I didn't have to turn around to know who it was. Throughout the rest of my shift, Mr. Tall, Dark, and, Handsome and I had played a silent game of seduction. A quick brush of my bare arm against his sleeve as I delivered his drink. The stroke of his fingers along the top of my hand as he set a chip on my tray. Was I interested? Yes, but not in my own casino, my own backyard.

He played blackjack steadily, following the dealer

as she moved through her rotation, as if he was convinced she was bringing him his luck. It took him out of my section, not that it made much difference. We kept an eye on one another. It got so I could tell when he was watching me, a feeling like cool air moving across my skin.

"You've never seen anyone do what?" I asked now, and felt him move to stand beside me.

"Daydream at night."

I turned my head to look at him. He was staring at the leap and play of the water, his face in profile. Again, I saw the contrast between his lean, sharp features and that rich, full mouth. Tension began to pool in my belly.

Definitely worth breaking the rules for, I thought.

"That's a nice thing to say," I said, my tone light.

He turned to look at me then, and I could see the way his eyes were dancing with mischief.

"I can be nice."

I laughed. It was such an obvious thing to say.

"Can I ask you something?" he went on.

"Sure," I said.

"What's your name?"

"Candace. Candace Steele," I replied.

I extended one hand in introduction. He took it, but instead of shaking it, he brought my hand to his lips, his eyes on mine. Now, finally, I felt that mouth against my skin. First the lips, then the slow glide of his tongue across my knuckles. Goose bumps danced across my skin. I felt a tug, deep in my groin.

"I'm Nate Lawlor," he said. He kept my hand in his. His thumb made lazy circles in my palm, and I felt my breasts tighten. "Mind if I ask you something else?"

"Twenty questions," I said. "After that, I'm cutting you off."

He grinned, quick and wicked, and gave my hand a tug. Slowly, he began to pull me toward him. One step, then two, until our pelvises bumped.

"Do you like to *play* games, Candace?" he asked. "Or do you just like to watch?"

"Yes," I said.

He laughed then, head thrown back. I watched the way the muscles moved in the column of this throat. Unable to resist the impulse, no longer certain why I should, I took a step toward him, sliding my breasts along his chest, nuzzling at the base of his throat with my open mouth.

He brought his hands up to my face, lifting it, then kissed me, deep and hard. I felt the world narrow down. This man. This desire. This time. This night.

"Come home with me, Candace," he murmured against my lips. "I can play all sorts of games."

"Show me, Nate," I whispered back. "Show me how."

I'm not sure how long it took to reach his apartment. I wasn't exactly watching street signs. Nate drove a BMW convertible, slate gray, top down. The desert air slid across my skin like cool silk.

He held my hand as we walked to the door. Inside, Nate's apartment suited him to perfection. All cool, hard surfaces, stark and streamlined. Big picture windows looked out toward the mountains, the glass tinted against the glare of the sun. He released me, and I went to stand before them, my eyes on the lights of the city spreading out across the valley floor. I heard the flare of a match being lit. The air filled with the sharp tang of sulfur.

Behind me, Nate moved slowly through the room. Clusters of tall pillar candles sprang to life. Their scent was something I couldn't quite put a name to, spicy and exotic. Flickering through my senses as the candlelight danced across the room.

And then, suddenly, Nate was there, behind me. Running his hands across the back of my tight jeans, then sliding them around to the front. I bent forward slightly and began to shift from side to side, rubbing my soft curves against him. He made a sound, low in his throat. Shivers danced across the surface of my skin, skittered down my spine. I heard someone take a sobbing breath, and realized I was the one sobbing.

With a sound that was almost audible, his control snapped. His hands tightened in my hair as he brought my questing mouth to his, and plundered. I felt my knees begin to shake then buckle. Never taking his mouth from mine, he caught me up, took two steps, then lowered me onto the couch.

For a moment, he stood, still as the statue he resembled, eyes glittering as they gazed down.

I let one hand rest limply at my side, as if I lacked the strength to lift it, even to touch him. With the other, I reached and ran my nails up the back of his leg. I saw the way his body jerked, just once. Then he was covering me, mouth hungry on my breasts, tongue sliding along the length of my neck, teeth biting gently at one sensitive earlobe.

"You have no idea what I want to do to you. What I'm *going* to do to you, Candace," he whispered, his words a promise that sent shivers down my spine.

I had broken all my rules for this moment, too. The moment his needs overtook him and he forgot himself.

Quick as lightning, I brought up the hand I had let drop to the side of the couch. There was a flash of something even I couldn't quite see, though I knew damn well what it was.

"Actually, I think that's my line, Nate," I said.

And plunged the long, thin stake of silver into his back, driving it all the way through to his black and treacherous vampire's heart.